THE DRIVING PASSION

MURDERS

GENE EPSTEIN

The Driving Passion Murders
Published by Penn Oak Publishing

Copyright © Gene Epstein 2020
All rights reserved

Cover design: The Steve Williams Design Office
Edited by Alan Grayce
Author photograph by Marlene Epstein

Also by Gene Epstein

Lemon Juice: The Confessions of a
Used Car Dealer–a Metamorphosis

Dying for an Heir

I wish to dedicate this book to the love of my life since she was 15 years old and I was 16 years old, my wife Marlene; without her I could not exist.

Prologue

On a delightful spring day, Robert Snyder was admiring beautifully restored classic cars adjacent to the Philadelphia Art Museum. He thought about his teenaged years when he worked with automobiles like these. But, after acting school, his only somewhat successful job was the lead role as the murderer in an off-Broadway play, which closed after a mere few weeks run. He thought to himself: *How did I ever get myself involved in multiple murders? Was this déjà vu?*

Gene Epstein

Chapter 1

It was just a few days since the world news focused on the
failed rescue attempt of 52 United States Embassy hostages
held in Tehran that resulted in the deaths of eight U.S.
servicemen but here on a bright sunny day in Center City
Philadelphia the concentration was on the Grand Philadelphia
Antique and Classic Automobile Show.

Many years had passed since Robert had driven a 1957
Chevrolet Bel Air convertible. It seemed like it was a lifetime
ago. His dreams as a teenager were caught up with reality and
were never realized. Here he was, getting a firsthand look at
one of his dreams that went down the proverbial toilet. This
was Robert's first visit to the Grand Philadelphia Antique and
Classic Automobile Show. For several years he had noticed the
publicity for the automobile show in Fairmount Park
adjoining the Museum of Art but this was the only time that
he was interested enough to attend, never thinking in his
wildest dreams that it would lead to multiple murders.

There were well over 100 magnificent automobiles
lined up in perfect rows with their proud owners busy in
conversation with other enthusiasts. He was drawn to the row
of the 1950 cars as his mind temporarily drifted back to his

16th birthday. Donald, his eldest brother, had prepared him for his driver's test however, their parents wouldn't let Robert take the family Buick Roadmaster for the road test. They did not believe he was capable of driving at the young age of 16, never telling him what age he would have to be to gain permission to drive the family's car, except constantly being told "older."

That's when Robert first called his uncle Al Goodson. He was his mother's brother and always liked Robert who he also called "Bob" or "Robert." He told Bob that he would help him get his first car since he owned a used car lot on Dealers Row on Broad Street in North Philadelphia.

Robert asked him if he could borrow any car so that he could at least pass his driver's test. Uncle Al told Bob to come to his car lot after school and he would have his porter, Arnold, take him for his driver's license exam in one of his cars.

"If you pass your test the first time, I'll give you a part-time job here after school and on the weekends, Robert," Uncle Al said. Robert was thrilled. Al instructed Arnold, his tall, stately African-American porter about 30 years of age to take the 1952 Chevrolet out of stock. "It's got automatic transmission, Robert, so you'll have no problem driving it," Al said as he patted Bob on the back. "Thanks, Uncle Al. This means so much to me. I'll be very careful," he said with sincere gratitude.

Uncle Al wanted Arnold to sit next to Robert on the drive to the state police barracks so that he could help him get used to the car. After only a few minutes of driving, Bob took to it like his first experience on a bicycle. It was so much smaller than the family Roadmaster and the Powerglide automatic transmission was perfect for a beginner. Robert was in a cold sweat. His hands were shaking, but 15 minutes later it was like "old hat." Less than two hours later he had completed the examination and had passed with flying colors. Robert jumped for joy after the police officer placed the "PASSED" stamp on his learner's permit. So excited, Robert hugged Arnold. Arnold looked astonished with his eyes wide open. "Don't you do that to me again. No! No! Don't do that again. What do you think I am? Queer?" Robert was laughing at him with his surprised look. "Sorry, Arnold. I was just so happy that I passed the test the first time. Thank you so much for helping me," he said and looked relieved.

Once back at the car lot Uncle Al was happy to learn that Bob had passed his road test, "Just be here on time after school and I'll pay you minimum wage. Arnold will teach you how to make a piece of shit look like a diamond, "Al remarked.

"Uncle Al, I don't know how long it will take me to get here after school. I have to take the bus and then the subway then walk three blocks, but I'll get here as quickly as possible," he replied to Uncle Al.

"Don't worry Robert," Uncle Al said, "here's the keys and the owner's card. You drive it carefully and it's yours as long as you work here." Al said. "Don't screw up or you'll be walking rather than driving and you'll be out of work." He finished his commands as he smiled and handed Robert the keys.

"She's been restored to better than original condition. Each nut and bolt has been replaced from the ground up," said the owner of the '57 Chevy Bel Air that Robert was looking at.

He looked at the man with glassy eyes thinking about his aspirations as a youth which were never fulfilled.

***

Robert was the envy of most of the kids in his class to be driving a 1952 Chevy. Not that it was a flashy car. It was just plain as it could be; however, it was a car. Transportation...Freedom...Only a few of his classmates had cars back then. At home, they were borrowed from their parents for an occasional ride to school. Only one other kid took a car on a regular basis, Tom Eckinger. And he had the car that everyone dreamed about: a 1957 Chevrolet Bel Air convertible that was silver-gray with red vinyl and silver interior like this one at the car show that he was admiring. It was a gift from his wealthy parents. When he drove the car to school, everyone flocked to see him. Every kid had dreamed of owning a car like this.

4

"I never had a car like this when I was younger. It took me four years to get this together and a whole lotta money," mentioned the proud owner. "You won't find a better one anywhere," he continued as Robert looked into the rear seat of the car.

One Friday, after working at Al's Autorama for six weeks and doing a good job compounding and waxing the cars, Al had handed Robert his pay envelope. It was heavier than usual: inside were the keys to a '57 Chevrolet Bel Air convertible.

"You can use this tonight but it better get back here safe and sound if you ever want another chance to use it," Al commanded.

That evening Robert had a date with Joyce Anderson, a girl that he met in the school lunchroom. Joyce was a pretty girl with blond hair and blue eyes and was about 5' 3" tall. They liked each other from the first time they met standing in line waiting for lunch. From that time in the ninth grade through most of high school they were great friends and lovers.

At a park in the Chestnut Hill area named by both young and old as "Lover's Lane," Robert had driven his car down the gravel road leading from the park's split-rail entrance through some brush to find a place off the beaten path.

"Robert don't do that to me. Not here where someone can look in." Joyce cried out when they were making out in the backseat of the '57 Chevy.

***

"I bet many lovers used that seat over the years," the owner at the car show chirped.

"I'm sure they did," Robert replied as he snapped back to reality, coming back from the 50s. He walked to the next row of cars leaving the owner of the Chevy with his dreams until another memory hit him.

There it was... A gorgeous 1955 Jaguar Roadster displayed in handsome British racing green with a tan top and Bridge Weir tan leather seats. Years before that car was one of his Uncle Al's favorite. Robert was not even permitted to take Al's Jaguar Roadster to the gas station. Neither was Arnold. Every week Robert would wash the Jaguar thoroughly and apply another coat of wax, hand rubbed and polished even though it was spotless. The dashboard was replete with handsome walnut wood in which the gauges where inset. The car that Robert was looking at was every bit as nice as his Uncle Al's.

***

"Are you working or not, Robert?" Al startled him.

While Robert was applying leather conditioner to the seats, his mind drifted as he ruminated about being a movie star. Since being in a class play in junior high school, he had aspirations of being an actor. He got plenty of help watching his uncle Al come up with far-fetched stories when he sold his used cars. He was one of the few boys to take drama in high school and sought to continue in college. He thought someday he would be a famous actor.

The first summer working for Al went by quickly. He looked forward to working there the following summer while just managing to get passing grades at high school over the fall and winter. As the next summer approached he knew that in order to be accepted to college he would have to take additional courses in summer school to make up for his barely passing grades. Somehow, he managed a schedule with Al that still enabled him to work a full week at the car lot while attending early classes at summer school, which significantly increased his grades. Al was glad to see his nephew work hard at the car lot and do so well in school that he sold a 1949 Ford two-door coupe with a V-8 engine (that Al was asking $200 for) to Robert for only $50.

Robert, as most youths entering college, was uncertain what he would major in. A liberal arts track was the first step towards figuring out whether to become a lawyer —which meant extending his college education by years— or taking classes in drama. After being accepted to Temple University, Robert thought that he would love to be in the theatre; however, it made more sense to pursue law and eventually become a prosecutor or a criminal defense lawyer. He finished his academic studies near the top of his class and entered law school but then totally changed direction. Robert could never stop dreaming of becoming a famous actor and he dropped out of law school after his first year.

He then attended drama classes, which was a thrill of a lifetime for him. He paid more attention to all his instructors than ever before. This would be the threshold over which he had to pass to become a noted actor.

***

Robert's eyes opened wide as a 1954 Cadillac Eldorado convertible came through the entrance gates and parked in a line of prestige automobiles. Its white finish blend and tons of chrome sparkled in the sun showing off its massive front grille with bullets protruding like ramming rods. He walked up to get a closer look at the car as he peered through the driver's door only to hear: "Please sir," the owner's voice crackled, "don't touch the car! See the sign," he said, pointing to a very conspicuous sign.

"She's a one-owner with 35,000 original miles. You'll never find another one like her anywhere in the country."

Thoughts of which just had raced through Robert's mind.

"This was the finest Cadillac ever built. A real trouble-free car."

"Yes I know," Robert said as he continued walking on.

"Bob. Bob Snyder. Is that you?" a female voice rang out.

He turned around and hesitated at first looking into a crowd of people and manage to see a familiar face.

"Mandy. Mandy Roberson? I can't believe it's you! After all these years!" He reached out for her with open arms as they embraced. "Your perm threw me off."

"And you? When did this hippie ever go around wearing a smart suit? You were always wearing torn jeans and hair down to your shoulders," Mandy reacted.

"Look at you. Your sculptured face still would make a Greek goddess jealous," he said, looking at this woman who he had loved. "How are you, Mandy? It's been so long."

"First of all, I'm no longer Mandy Roberson. I am Amanda Dillington." She hesitated. "It's been a lifetime ago since our days at Temple. Who would ever have expected Robert Snyder to be the *bon vivant* looking and dressing like a self-made millionaire? What have you been doing for the past 20 years?"

"Let's grab a dog and a Coke like the good old days," he said and reached for her outstretched hand as they walked over to a nearby vendor. "Two hotdogs with extra sauerkraut," he ordered. When he got the order, he put on a heavy coat of mustard and handed one to Mandy. The two of them set down on the Victorian style wooden slatted bench and immersed themselves in conversation covering the past 20 years. Robert had very little to recap since his life had been pretty much uneventful.

Mandy had realized very shortly that Robert's ambitions were never realized and that he went through many periods of desperation, misery, and a definite lack of accomplishments. The only thing Amanda could ascertain that Robert had going for him lately, was a job at his uncle Al's car lot polishing cars.

She, on the other hand, had dropped out of drama class and had plunged head-on into a law career. She subsequently became an assistant district attorney in Philadelphia prosecuting trials of many headline cases. It was in her first year in the DAs office where she met the man she would ultimately marry, Clarkson Dillington III, who had recently been killed in an automobile accident.

They discussed the times when they both were hippies and going through a hot and heavy courtship. They thought that they held the answers to all the world's problems. Drugs were the scene, however, neither of them ventured into anything more powerful than marijuana during their 'flower child' period.

Robert's mind quickly focused on one particularly enjoyable day having sex with Mandy in a vacant second-floor classroom at Temple. They both had the same finance class; however, for some reason, the professor only showed for the first day of the semester. All the students in the class were told to read their books and they could be assured of getting a B. The teacher never returned, thus the classroom was virtually empty as the other students relaxed around Mitten Hall.

One morning after having breakfast on campus Robert became completely aroused when Mandy gave him her most passionate kiss. Instead of going to Mitten Hall with the other students, Robert suggested that they both meet at the empty classroom. He arrived just moments before Mandy and had already lit up a joint. He was inhaling a few drags when Mandy entered. He had an erection which was throbbing in his pants. This was obvious to Mandy as she reached down and unzipped his fly. She took a third hit on the joint and as she did, Robert pulled her to the floor and reached beneath her skirt to find that she had been wearing nothing else. Both of them stripped off their clothes and Robert inserted himself deep into her as they both let out passionate screams as they were reaching an erotic climax.

Once finished, finding himself still erect and Mandy wanting more, he guided her on to the teacher's desk where they had sexual intercourse again. Mandy's erotic screaming caused someone to try to enter the classroom but Robert had locked it from the inside. Mandy looked frightened; however, that quickly wore off when Robert yelled to whoever was on the other end of the door, "Class is closed; get the fuck out."

She said that she was worried, but Robert said to her "Who gives a shit?"

A few minutes later both had put their clothes back on and unlocked the classroom door to find ten students standing there waiting for the next class. They looked at each other and laughed.

The noise of a car door slamming brought Robert back to the present. He took Amanda by the hand like an old buddy and walked her through the lanes of cars.

"They were great times. Weren't they? "Robert asked of Mandy.

"Times change," she replied. "You know nothing stays the same. Are you married?"

"No. Not even going with anyone," he answered.

After looking at dozens of other automobiles they both seemed lost for words and less interested in the automobiles that they came to see. Their worlds were diametrically opposed. From a beautiful sunny day the first Sunday in May, the skies turned quickly to grey with one or two ominous clouds approaching fast. All eyes were on the sky as car owners rushed to protect their 'gems' with various covers while the public scattered to get out of the rain.

Robert and Amanda looked at each other, shrugging their shoulders as if to ask, "Are you going?"

Just when Robert thought she was looking to leave, she said "Come on, we can get shelter at my place and I'll even prepare dinner. I live at 1700 Rittenhouse Place. We can be there before the storm hits." Amanda told him where her car was parked and that he could follow since she had valet parking on site.

Minutes later Robert drove his Buick sedan following right behind Amanda. She had a new Mercedes Benz S Class 500 sedan which was jet black with tan interior.

A doorman stood at attention wearing maroon livery, while an elderly porter opened the driver's side door and took her keys. There was ample space beneath the portico for Robert to be protected from the rain, which had picked up in intensity. All of a sudden a black Mercedes limousine pulled up with the license plate "ROY O" on the front. A crowd of people rushed around the automobile. Getting out of the automobile was a man dressed in black and wearing black sunglasses. Three people accompanied him as they all walked to the elevators. Robert thought, *Roy Orbison?*

He then asked the Porter if that was Roy Orbison and all the porter would say "It is his car," without ever confirming it.

Robert offered to park his car himself but the porter just stood there waiting for him to hand over the keys. He wasn't prepared for the luxury of having one's own porter and definitely wasn't prepared for what was to come.

The Driving Passion Murders

The doorman greeted Amanda with a smile and bent his head down while reaching for the brim of his hat acknowledging her appearance. He opened the door and also tipped his hat for Robert.

Once through the doorway, he could not stop looking in every direction of the lobby as he soaked in the majestic tall walls covered with deep walnut raised panels. They appeared to be thirty feet tall. In the center of a coffered ceiling hung massive crystal chandeliers, each nearly ten feet in diameter and nearly as tall. Arranged in an orderly fashion, were kid glove-soft leather sofas and club chairs in deep maroon. People were being served tea and pastries by butlers, while several were absorbed in reading, others seemed to be enjoying tête-à-tête conversations. Directly opposite the entrance were multiple elevators whose doors were works of art. They appeared to be brass with stainless steel appliqué. Bob was in awe of the craftsmanship of the metal vines intertwined from the bottom of each door to the top with flowers on both ends.

Amanda knew it would be a shock for Robert to see her opulent surroundings as she noticed him gazing in every direction as if he were young boy first attending his major league baseball game.

Once inside the elevator, Amanda told him, "This is what happened when I married the third generation of Dillingtons. Not really my cup of tea to be honest with you, but I have grown accustomed to it."

The next sound Bob heard was, "Penthouse, Mrs. Dillington," which came out of nowhere. Robert had no idea what to expect.

As Robert and Amanda exited the elevator to her Penthouse, he was picturing what Dorothy must have felt when she entered OZ. Robert couldn't speak. He was lost for words gazing through the skylight of the most spacious surroundings he could envision anyone living it. He was glad that the weather prediction for a sunny clear day was wrong as the rains continued to bounce off the skylight panels.

"Can I give you a tour?" Amanda asked.

Robert replied, "Yes, please. Please do."

"The flooring here in the foyer and living room is Jerusalem tile but a pain for the housekeeper to keep spotless. Off to either side leading into the dining room are ¾-inch walnut planks from the excess flooring from Joseph Napoleon Bonaparte's home in Bordentown, New Jersey."

"Whew!" Robert exclaimed.

"I still don't really care for the old furniture in the dining room," Amanda pointed out. "They are from Clarkson's grandparents. All Chippendale, that's why I mixed in other odds and ends. I didn't want this to be a museum so Clarkson agreed and had presented me with various photographs by modernists furniture makers for my approval."

"I really love that dining room table and chairs myself. I could really handle everything that is here," Robert said.

"Some Bucks County artist that built JFK's desk, built that years ago for Clarkson. I think his name was Whitley or Whitaker or something like that," she remarked. "I'm trying to remember, but it's slipped my mind. The ten cherry chairs are Philadelphia Chippendale."

"These gold chairs," she added as she caressed one of them, "are from Salvatore Dali's designs that I love. They break up the boredom of the old furniture."

Yet on the walls surrounding the dining room set were pop art works done by none other than Andy Warhol. Not reproductions mind you, but by his own hand. Like a child in a candy store, Robert was astonished at the luxury. No matter in which direction he looked, there was beauty that he never envisioned before. Magnificent artworks and gorgeous furniture in an enormous apartment with five bedrooms even though they had no children. All that Robert could think was that they must've entertained plenty of people who had either too much to drink or too many drugs to safely go home.

Every room that Robert walked into had some type of significance to Amanda's deceased husband or from generations that preceded him. He could sense that Mandy was trying to put her touches to this gorgeous apartment to make her feel comfortable. But no matter how she tried, she was still living in the Dillingtons' presence.

Flashing through Robert's mind numerous times was seeing how Amanda is living now and what he had done wrong all the years of his life to be nearly destitute.

After floundering for many years with low paying acting roles and getting minimal advances to pay his rental, he received a call from Bill Spaulding, his agent, friend, confidant, and a prominent attorney.

"What do you have for me, Bill? A good part, finally? Is it *Les Miserable*? Theater? Movies? Commercials? What?"

William Aaron Spaulding from the Law firm of Calhoun, Spaulding, and Finegold replied, "No, nothing like that. But I might be able to get you out of this deep rut that you are in. Do you know how much I have advanced you over the past few years? It's payback time. Can you meet me at the Palm restaurant on Broad Street this afternoon for lunch?" Bill asked. "Sure. Give me directions and I'll be there," stated Robert.

"Now sit down while I explain," said Bill. "I've been branching out into other fields since this Broadway crap and movies is for the birds. My clients seldom do well, as you perfectly know. You are not alone. Everybody wants to make it big in theater and movies and there are a million dreamers out there like you waiting for the big break. Then, there is the reality when you finally have to wake up and say to yourself that you've been lying to yourself. I've been handling some choice estates and I thought with your education and acting experience you might want to get a fresh start and a place for yourself in life."

"What in the world are you talking about?" Bob inquired.

"Simply this. I represent an elderly widow who is childless and in need of someone to help her with her day-to-day responsibilities. Someone to bring her the newspaper. Someone to hire a groundskeeper for her luxurious estate.

Someone to watch over her. She is a lovely lady, however, life's daily tasks are getting too much for her. She needs someone to write out her checks and see that her house is kept up. Someone like the son that she never had. Is that clear? "

"You want me to be a babysitter?" Bob said.

"Yes, if necessary, and a companion. If you get the job it will pay you $750.00 a week clear plus a beautiful apartment on the property and the use of a car. All your food and clothing will be provided for you by the estate and all of your utilities included. Now tell me what have you been offered that is better in the past ten years?"

Bob was speechless. For one thing, he did not have any money at all. For the past several months he's been sleeping in a friend's filthy apartment. He owed his friend. He owed all his friends. But more than anyone he owed Bill. Bill had represented Bob for nearly ten years, getting him worthless parts where there were none at all for one whose ability was at the lower part of the scale as was Bob's. He knew it and Bill's reality check struck home.

"OK, I'll take the job." Bob responded.

Bill stopped him in his footsteps. "Not so quick. There's more to it than just accepting this position. I have a fiduciary responsibility to my client to advertise for the position and thoroughly check out those that apply to be certain that person has impeccable credentials and has proven to be responsible and caring. I am positive that there will be many applicants for such a sought-after position. I will interview those that apply and I will advise her on the one that I think is the most qualified, however, since I've known you so well for decades, I may recommend to my client that she place you in her employ."

"What do you mean you may recommend your client to hire me? I thought that's what you wanted me to do to start with." Bob was now raising his voice.

"Well Bob, there is still this: Mrs. Moore has been diagnosed with a brain tumor. She might not last too long. A close friend is important to her now, especially one who looks after her every need. She has an estate worth millions of dollars which includes rare furnishings, artworks and a few antique automobiles. I believe that with my orchestration and you playing the role of your lifetime, I may be able to get you placed in the estate leaving you a sizable sum whenever she passes on. As I told you she has no children and very few relatives, none of whom have ever offered her any acts of kindness or compassion," he continued. "You owe me quite a tidy sum if I added up all those years helping you financially through one trying time after another. Years ago when I originally signed to represent you we had agreed that all sums advanced to you and all costs that I incurred were not only due back in full but additionally giving me a one-third percentage of your future income. I will request now that you sign a personal contract with me reaffirming everything and giving me one-third of your net worth in cash to pay me back when you are in a financial position to do so. This way whenever Mrs. Moore expires, whether it is next year or several years from now, should you be the beneficiary, whether partial or sole, you will owe me one third in cash immediately. No hesitations! No excuses. Do you realize what that can amount to for you? By the way, if she approves of you, I want you to give me the antique cars as a bonus for all that I have and am doing for you. Is it a deal?"

Bob sat there absorbing everything that his dearest friend Bill was saying and then he queried, "How long might she live and would I be assured of a job if she lives many years? How would I know if I was placed in her will?"

Bill assured him that if he does his job well, he would do everything to influence Mrs. Moore to agree. Then Bill reached into his pocket and handed Bob $500.00 in hundred-dollar bills with the instructions to buy a new suit, shirts, and shoes.

"Look clean and respectable and shave that 5-day growth. Get a close haircut."

That was enough for Bob to shake hands with his agent-attorney and to confirm, "Yes, we have a deal."

Chapter 2

Walking through Center City, Robert passed a few boutique eateries that had recently opened but would probably close within three years. He came across an impressive men's clothing store that was housed beautifully within the confines of an early twentieth century bank. As he entered the hallowed halls of yesteryear's luxurious bank his eyes immediately focused on a magnificent center hall marble staircase reminiscent of the staircase from *Gone With the Wind'*, replete with intricately designed balusters and handrails leading to a second-floor shop.

"Can I help you, sir?" a cordial diminutive salesman asked Bob, who replied that he wished to find a nice suit and shirt. "Please walk with me." As they ascended the staircase, Bob was wondering how much the clothes cost here. He was soon to find out.

The salesman showed him several suits. "You look to be a size 42 regular. Am I correct?"

"I've been 175 pounds for most of my adult life and my last suit was a size 42." Bob looked for the price on the reverse side of the tag attached to the end of the sleeve. "Honestly, I cannot afford this. I have $500.00 to purchase a suit, tie, shirt and shoes."

The salesman seemed surprised at Bob's honesty. He was probably used to hearing other excuses. "We can get you a line of credit if you so desire since it seems like you like this suit." The salesman held the jacket open for Bob to try on. Looking in the mirror Bob smiled.

"Let me try on the pants to see how everything looks."

The salesman looked pleased.

Standing at 6' 1" with his black hair pulled back into a short ponytail that would soon disappear, his brown eyes opened wide, Robert liked the vision of his new self, dressed in a dark blue suit with a white shirt with blue pinstripes and a button-down collar with a red tie. "Let's do it!"

"Not until our finest tailor makes sure that this fit is perfect. No one is better than Charles. He has been with our company for 35 years."

"I was going to ask you which side you dress on, Mr. Snyder, however, I can see quite well that it is on your left," Charles, the baldheaded master tailor stated.

The salesman escorted Bob to the first floor to fill out a basic bank credit application. Since Bob never had a loan nor had any steady income to show, it proved fruitless to get the bank to approve it. However, since he had nearly 50% to put down, the company agreed to approve the loan in-house with a repayment plan over six months. Bob was told that his suit would be ready to pick up the following morning as a special favor to him by his salesman. Next, to get a haircut from a barber and not at his own hand.

The weather was bright and sunny so Bob leisurely walked around Center City looking for a franchise hair cutting establishment since their prices were usually lower than most. He stopped by a vendor's cart and got a hot dog with sauerkraut that he covered heavily in mustard. As everyone does, he kept enjoying his sandwich while entering 'Cutz for U'. Less than 25 minutes later Bob's hair was professionally styled eliminating his ponytail and giving him a clean looking appearance. Bob actually liked what was happening.

The following day Bob tried on his new suit, shirt and tie and everything fit to his delight. He handed over the remainder of his $500.00 after signing the loan documents and was bid farewell by both the salesman and Charles the tailor.

***

"Get today's *Inquirer* and open up the classified section. Then call the phone number in the advertisement immediately and state that you are applying for the job that is advertised," were Bill Spaulding's instructions. "This has to appear totally proper. My new secretary has already received four inquiries."

***

"Good afternoon. This is Robert Snyder. I'm applying for the position that you are offering in the *Philadelphia Inquirer*. I certainly have the credentials for such a position and I would like to make an appointment with whoever is handling this position."

"Mr. Spaulding is interviewing this week for the position. When would you like to come in Mr. Snyder? I can see if Mr. Spaulding has an opening," Darlene the secretary spoke.

"Please tell me the most convenient time for Mr. Spaulding, as my schedule is totally flexible," Bob responded.

"Tomorrow at 2 o'clock is definitely open if that works for you, Mr. Snyder?"

"Count on me being there promptly at 2 pm." She gave him the directions to the building and his office suite number not realizing that he had been there previously.

***

Bill Spaulding sat at his desk with his feet up, reclining in his high-back leather chair as Robert entered. "Sit down," he commanded and without hesitation, Robert pulled up one of the three chairs in front of Bill's spacious mahogany desk with each leg emblazoned with gold appearing appliqués.

"Is the job mine?"

"You certainly look like a different person. Not the one that I remember in our decades of friendship." Bill continued, "You are the fourth person to apply in person for the position and I'm glad to tell you that I wholeheartedly have recommended you to Mrs. J.P. Moore. I will personally drive you to her estate in the Gladwyne suburbs this Saturday be here at my office at 10 a.m. since I've arranged a personal interview at 11 AM. Any questions?"

"Thank you, Bill. I will be early. Should I follow you with my car so that I can leave from there?" Robert asked.

"No, we will take my car since we will have to discuss things further or our return if she likes you," replied Bill.

***

Saturday came and Bill pressed a button and told his secretary to have his car brought to the front door of the building."

"Which car Mr. Spaulding?"

"The sedan," he quipped. "I wish that Selma was still here. I can't deal with breaking in a new secretary." Bill appeared upset that his former secretary had been diagnosed with her second bout of breast cancer and was receiving multiple treatments which weakened her too much to come into work.

Bill's desk phone rang from the garage. "Which black sedan Mr. Spaulding?"

"My Goddam Mercedes!" he screamed.

Both Bill Spaulding and Robert took the elevator down to the ground floor and his car was waiting with the porter holding open the driver's door for Attorney William Spaulding.

"Good afternoon, Henry," Bill acknowledged the porter.

"Good afternoon to you, Mr. Spaulding. I hope that you have a wonderful day." As Bill seated himself, the porter closed the door.

"Take this," Bill handed Robert the printout directions from Center City. "These are AAA directions to Mrs. Moore's

19

Gene Epstein

for the future if she approves of you. Take Benjamin Parkway, Kelly Drive and I-76 West to Harrow Lane in Upper Kellington Township. Take exit 337 from Interstate 76 West. Take exit 337 towards Gladwyne. Twenty-six minutes and 11.9 miles."

On the way there, Bill gave Robert some background information on Mrs. Jacquelin Phyllis Moore. "She was the hostess of hostesses constantly having parities at their estate 'Hampton Court' until her husband died three years ago. She had a fall and broke her right hip which never healed properly even after two operations. She is 80 years old, mentally bright and mobile most of the time but when she gets stressed or tired she uses a cane or even her wheelchair. For several months after her surgery, I arranged to have a retired nurse there to help her continue to do the physical therapy that her orthopedic surgeon had recommended since she was lax in doing it herself. She has a housekeeper, Stasha, who barely speaks English but comes in a several days a week to keep the house neat and also will take care of your apartment. The nurse is no longer there since Mrs. Moore wasn't improving and refused any additional P.T. Any questions?"

Before long they arrived at Mrs. Moore's. There was an impressive Art Deco wrought iron double gate that was attached to a pair of eight-foot-high stone pillars. On the face of each pillar recessed in the stonework were raised letters with a gold finish on black metal background spelling out 'Hampton Court.' Bill had the remote gate opener but, as always, called Mrs. Moore on the intercom phone inset in a stainless-steel box within the stone pillar or, depending on where he was, would use the car telephone set in the center console.

"My dear. It is Bill with the person that I spoke to you about. I am coming in now," he said as he then depressed the remote and the gates opened inwardly welcoming them.

"Come in," she replied as they drove down the cobblestone driveway to park at the carriage house. The carriage house itself was very impressive with eight wood garage doors that were stained a handsome mahogany, each with two rows of glass windows about 10 by 12 inches

20

separated by thick mullions and above eye level to let natural light enter. The building was in fieldstone with grey slate roof. It was two stories tall with a full apartment above the garage area. To the right of the carriage house down a serpentine flagstone path barely one hundred feet was Hampton Court's main house. To each side of the path were manicured flower beds and security lights to light the path in darkness. Upon reaching the main entrance was a wide handsome mahogany door with raised panels, an antique from a historic English manor.

Before Bill could raise the heavy iron lion's head door knocker, Mrs. Moore opened the door. She was leaning a bit on a cane. Mrs. J.P. Moore didn't look her 80 years of age. She was dressed as if she were going to dinner at a fine restaurant. She was made up and looked as though she was ready for a good time. Her hair was brushed back and up in a French bun. Aside from the cane and an obvious difficulty walking this woman looked the very bright and cheerful and greeted them both very warmly giving Bill a hug and a kiss on each cheek.

"Mrs. Moore, this is Robert Snyder," introduced Bill.

"Billy. Please. I'm not your ordinary client. We've known each other for years. Please call me Jackie." she requested. Being the hostess that she was, she simply gestured with a graceful wave of her left hand to enter the living room.

"Your home is magnificent, Mrs. Moore," stated Robert. "May I ask how old this house is?"

"It originally dated back to William Penn's days when this was 200 acres but over the years, parcels were sold off and my husband's family purchased it about 100 years ago. Since we moved here it seems like we have been updating it every year up until my husband recently passed away."

"Tell me, Robert, what do your friends call you?" she asked.

"It's a toss-up, Mrs. Moore. Some call me Bob and others Robert."

"I like Robert. If you don't mind that is what I shall call you," Mrs. Moore's stated.

"Now, Robert. Tell me what you have done in the past that you would want to work here for me?"

"My mother's friend lost her son in a tragic accident and she was in an awful state. She went through several people who had attended to her but was upset that they only sat on their backsides and claimed they did nothing except smoke cigarettes or steal her liquor. None lasted more than a few days, possibly a week. While I was going to college, I was asked to help out for a week or two; however, she kept asking me to stay on, which I did but I had other plans. I was a student at Temple's drama department and was torn between doing both. Eventually, she moved in with her niece and nephew in Palm Beach."

Bill was shocked. Of all things, the most obvious was that he hadn't gone over Robert's background. Bill looked surprised at Robert's ease in making up the entire story.

"Mrs. Moore...pardon me—'Jackie'. I had my people do a thorough check on Robert and we found him to be very sincere with no vices."

"Oh Billy, everybody has some vices or life wouldn't be any fun," smiled Mrs. Moore. "Come let me show you around while I still have my energy."

Without discussing any of the duties that would be Robert's responsibility, Mrs. Moore took Robert for a tour of her home starting with the living room area, where she pointed to an old carved marble fireplace mantle that stood on white marble arches with a keystone in the center. She showed him the pictures sitting on top of the mantle of her parents and her husband's ancestors. Robert paid attention to everything that she said while at the same time admiring this woman who did her best to stand upright even though she was in obvious pain as she leaned on her cane. She pointed out that the room was kept as it was originally built with its white plaster ceiling and exposed 3" x 12" wood beams that were stained a deep natural color and ran the width of this large room. The walls were plastered and painted a light lime color that had six pairs of floor-to-ceiling windows, two of which framed doors that opened to the gardens. Imported 19th century drapes in solid sky blue gracefully bordered each opening. The furnishings in the room were elegant and period correct and enhanced with occasional oil paintings by Samuel Alken Sr., the renowned English artist, illustrating his favorite hunt scenes to give this room a true museum appearance.

Leaving the living room Mrs. Moore walked through an arched hall leading to the dining room. The dining room was very similar in layout and taste as the living room. In the center was a dining room table that would seat 16 people. The table, that had been constructed for Mr. Moore's parents, was nearly 100 years old. The table was made of walnut planks that were cut down from trees on their estate. Standing like soldiers were 16 chairs with a golden embroidered cloth material on the cushions and backrests. The finish on the table shined like glass. In pointing out the table to Robert and her attorney she said that this room has not been used for nearly a decade and that she would rather have her meals in the anteroom adjacent to the kitchen. For that reason, she refused to have the 16 place settings of dishes and silverware on the table since that would mean only more things to keep clean. However, there were two beautiful silver candelabras placed to the right and left of the center of the table.

At this point, Mrs. Moore seemed a little bit exhausted and instructed Bill to "please show Robert the accommodations for him."

In Robert's mind, it seemed as though Mrs. Moore had accepted him for the job and he smiled. Not even knowing or thinking if anyone saw him smile, it was something he could not hold back. He liked her along with her sense of humor and determination do not let anything stand in her way as long as she could.

"I'll show Robert the accommodations should you both agree," and waved his right hand to Robert after he first made sure that Mrs. Moore was comfortably seated.

"I think she sincerely likes you, Robert. I'm very happy for that," said Bill. "I have the keys, so follow me."

They exited the main house and walked down the flagstone path to the carriage house. Bill opened the entrance door and only a few steps inside were stairways that led to the second floor and a door to the right that led to the six-car garage.

As Robert anxiously placed his right hand on the rail leading to the second floor Bill abruptly stopped him. "Wait. I want to see the cars again."

Using one of his keys, he unlocked the door to the right then turned on the switch for the interior lighting of the carriage house garage. Bill was in awe for he had a love of old cars since childhood. He used to sketch them. He used to dream about them. He used to make his own designs hoping that someday someone would build a car to his drawings.

"Do you know what you're looking at? " he asked Robert.

"I sure do. There is a '54 Eldorado convertible like my uncle used to have. I see that she has a rare 1955 or 1956 Gullwing Mercedes 300. I used to work for my uncle who sold these from his car lot when I was a kid. Wow! Look at that gorgeous 1932 Duesenberg Model J with a supercharger."

Before Robert continued to show that he understood that there were some very beautiful and desirable antique automobiles Bill stopped him in his tracks.

"Let me show you the apartment where you're going to be living." Bill directed Robert to follow him upstairs.

At the top of the stairs were a hat and coat rack made from deer antlers and a seat to put one's boots on during inclement weather. Once the door was opened a switch turned some dim lights on a kitchen table and a hallway. The interior was totally different from the main house. It had a rustic theme that carried throughout the apartment. When you entered you were immediately in a very airy kitchen even though it was small in size. The ceiling with a tall A-frame with heavy wooden beams crossing the room. From the peak of the 'A' ceiling hung a carriage wheel lamp with six electrified kerosene lanterns. To the right was a television room which in reality was a small living room . There were antique rifles and shotguns on the walls and electrified oil lamps on the end tables and a sofa made of mixed leather hides in a large diamond pattern. Between the kitchen and the television room was a short hallway leading to a bathroom on the left that was modern and had a bathtub fitted with shower doors. One bedroom to the right with a double bed and a tall dresser and a sliding door closet that had a mirror facing to help make the bedroom appear larger. The opposite bedroom had a single bed with a night table on either side. Neatly placed on each wall were other Samuel Alken Sr.'s fox hunting scenes however all were smaller than those hanging in the main house .

"Bill, I really owe you. You came through for me once again. I love this place and Mrs. Moore seems like a doll." Robert said, his voice showing his excitement.

He added, "Do you think that she is offering me the position?"

"You would've been gone a half-hour ago if she had any unsure feelings about you. Mrs. Moore is totally upfront with everyone. At her age, she doesn't stand on ceremony." Bill answered. "Let's go back to the house and firm things up."

Retracing their steps back to the main house Bill approached the front door and tapped the Lion's Head knocker twice, then opened the door himself realizing that Mrs. Moore would be expecting them. In the living room, he found her resting on a Victorian chaise lounge with her eyes closed. Her hearing was not affected by her age and she heard them enter. She quickly sat up and stated, "I was just resting with my eyes closed," since her vanity would not permit anyone to think she might have dozed off.

She presented a list of things that she expected to have Robert carry out. Some items were marked to do or check daily and others marked weekly or monthly. Nothing came as a surprise to Robert, nor was there anything difficult to do. Most items were those which would be performed by an administrator. Others were minor such as running errands, bringing in the mail and going over invoices and utility bills for her estate.

"Would you like your paycheck weekly or monthly, Robert?"

"Whatever your pleasure, Mrs. Moore. I'm here to do whatever you need and to do it well," he gratefully answered.

"Oh, it's a moot point, Robert, since once you get acclimated you will be writing all the checks. My hand cannot write legibly since this damn 'Essential tremor' I inherited from the generations that preceded me. All I can do is scribble my initials." she hesitated. "Now, how soon can you start?"

Chapter 3

Within a few days, Robert knew the routine and had her breakfast ready for her at 9:15 sharp: three scrambled eggs very loose and runny with four pieces of bacon, Florida orange juice and two pieces of lightly toasted white bread. He walked down the long driveway every day at 1 o'clock to bring in the mail and sort what might be personal mail that he would hand directly to Mrs. Moore and throw out the junk mail. On his desk in the study, he had one incoming and one outgoing file that was made of dark oak where neatly organized bills were placed.

His desk was a deep oak-stained serpentine 1920's circa roll-top that housed numerous cubbyholes at the far end of the desk and in the base to the right and the left of the leg opening were very heavy drawers that had to be pulled with some amount of difficulty. Robert rubbed a heavy coat of beeswax on the runners to make it easier.

After going through the bill, he sorted them for the estate purposes and personal items. Robert came under estate items and her groceries, which he picked up twice a week along with her orders from her favorite butcher in town, would be filed under personal. A few days after Robert started, Mrs. Moore had her banker come over with papers to put Robert on the checking account. She had two accounts. One account for personal items and the other for expenses related to the estate. He had authorization for both accounts, however, they were capped at $500. Anything over $500 Robert would need Mrs. Moore's signature in addition to his. This was the advice that her banker gave her and she took.

Robert had a meeting with Victor, a young man about 30 years old, who was born and raised in Guatemala. He had worked faithfully for her for the past ten years and knew everything that had to be done for the grounds work. Even though half of his life was spent in the United States one would think that he just arrived for it was so difficult for him to understand instructions. He would constantly nod his head as if he understood but Robert soon discovered that he would have to ask Victor to tell him what he had just said. Victor also worked taking care of two neighbors' properties within a mile of Hampton Court and found other work over the wintertime when the grounds did not need maintenance helping do tile work for a contractor.

Every week Robert would go into the carriage house garage and start each automobile. Every other week each car would be taken out for a 20-minute drive which was the minimum time that an automobile needed to be warmed up sufficiently so that all the lubricants did their job. This was really fun 'work' for Robert. He felt like he was working at his uncle Al's car lot when he was a kid. He knew everything about the white 1954 Cadillac Eldorado convertible but this was a one-owner car with only 35,000 miles. Mr. Moore had purchased it new and it still had most of its original paint with the exception of some minor paint work to one door when Mrs. Moore opened it not realizing that she was too close to a parking lot signpost. It still had its original black convertible top; however, the back-plastic window had turned brown over the years. He would see if a local upholstery shop would be competent to replace it. The interior of the car surprised him the most. Under wool blankets that loosely covered the seats were supple leather seats in red and white that looked like they were never sat on.

Adjacent to the Cadillac was the 1956 Mercedes 300 SL Silver grey Gullwing 2-seater with red leather bucket seats. He could not believe that it showed only 9000 miles but it did for sure.

"This should be in a museum," he said to himself. "They only built 311 of these."

He then looked closely at the 1932 Duesenberg in a handsome burgundy finish with a tan top and tan leather interior. It had a badge on the front bumper indicating that it was a National ACD First place winner in 1969 in Auburn, Indiana. As he looked closer he knew he was looking at yet another magnificent automobile. In the glove compartment, he found award badges from national events around the country.

Someone had performed an incredible restoration on this, went through his mind.

Before going any further Robert heard a buzzer and then the voice of Mrs. Moore through an intercom system. "Robert, can you come to the house?"

He looked up and said, "I'll be there immediately," without even knowing if Mrs. Moore heard him since he was unfamiliar with the system. He rushed to the main house and Mrs. Moore was standing at the doorway resting on her cane. "Robert, it is such a beautiful day today. How about taking me for a walk around the grounds?" She pointed to her wheelchair, which Robert immediately brought over to her and gently assisted her to sit comfortably.

"I'm here to serve you, Mrs. Moore. It is my pleasure and my honor."

He guided the wheelchair down the walkway past the carriage house to the garden.

"Let me just get some sun and you do whatever you would like," she told Robert.

"I would be glad to sit here with you if you don't mind, Mrs. Moore." He meant every word of it because he was really caring about this woman especially since he never had a warm nor caring relationship with his mother.

As the days turned into weeks he was enjoying this position more than he ever thought. Then one day after road testing and gassing up her classic cars, he had an idea. He came into the house but he left the Cadillac Eldorado outside.

"Mrs. Moore, I'm taking you to dinner. It's on me. You've told me many times how you and your husband used to go to Blue Bell Inn for dinner once a week. Will you let me take you?"

"Oh, Robert! You have no idea what a thrill that would be for me to have dinner with you there; however, my dear boy, you cannot afford to pay for it and I am certain that our old house account is still viable," she said.

"We are taking the Cadillac convertible, if you don't mind," he informed her.

"My husband used to take me there in his Rolls Royce sedan that he purchased new in 1965," stated Mrs. Moore.

***

At 5 o'clock, after pushing the wheelchair to the Cadillac and making certain that she was seated comfortably, they were on their way. Less than 30 minutes later they pulled up to the parking lot of the Blue Bell Inn and as Robert guided the wheelchair towards the entranceway she looked up to the roof and she saw the owner's sister, Dorothy, repairing shingles on the roof. "That's Dorothy. She does everything here," Mrs. Moore exclaimed. Less than 20 minutes later Dorothy would be serving liver pâté and fried oysters at the bar for both of them.

Dorothy came over to give Mrs. Moore a hug and kiss. Mrs. Moore was so thrilled to see Dorothy for it had been several years since she last had a dinner there which she terribly missed.

After a wonderful dinner and cocktails, Robert drove Mrs. Moore home and helped her to her bedroom while he turned the lights down leaving just one hallway light on for her as he retired to his apartment.

***

It wasn't long before this became a weekly event that both Mrs. Moore and Robert looked forward to.

"Mrs. Moore. I see on the calendar that you have an appointment in two days with your oncologist. I just wanted to remind you," Robert stated. He had remembered Bill telling him that she was dying and it was only a matter of time. Bill never went into whatever the disease was, only that it was serious. Robert was so happy in his new position that afforded him a wonderful place to live and a nice income with a closet filled with Brooks Brothers suits complementary of the estate plus a modern car to drive that he never inquired nor would he ask her what the serious ailment was. He had assumed that it was related to her broken hip and subsequent operations.

***

Two days later arriving at the Hospital of the University of Pennsylvania for her semi-annual checkup Robert located Dr. Goldstein on the third floor and pressed the elevator button to three. He guided the wheelchair to the waiting room and within ten minutes her name was called." Dr. Goldstein will see you now, Mrs. Moore," said the office secretary who was seated behind a sliding privacy window.

Sitting in the office about ten minutes later a very young-looking Dr. Goldstein entered.

"How are you feeling, Jackie? You look better than the last time that you were here. Are you taking some miracle drug that I'm not familiar with?" the doctor said in jest.

"No, Dr. Goldstein. I'm still taking the same medication for the past year perhaps it's because Robert has been taking such good care of me?"

The doctor was taking her blood pressure while his nurse was waiting to draw blood for testing. "As you know, I scheduled you for current MRI to see how much, if at all, the tumor has changed. They are waiting for you downstairs, but honestly Jackie, you look better than you did on your last visit. Do you feel any more pressure on your head? Has it gotten worse?" queried the doctor.

"The pressure seems the same. No improvement but I don't feel that it has progressed," she informed him.

Less than ten minutes later Dr. Goldstein told her that he would let her know what the blood tests showed and that whatever she's doing she could keep it up. He bent over and kissed her on the forehead and said, "I hope that the MRI shows no change."

"He is young but somehow he is keeping me alive," she proudly stated to Robert. And so are you, Robert. Now let's go down for another clanking of that MRI machine."

Robert did not know what to say if anything. He liked her so much that he wanted to continue to be part of her life. He totally enjoyed this new position and forgot about his desire to be a great actor. He quietly prayed that she would be fine. He also was upset that not one of her relatives ever contacted her to see how she was doing. Not a phone call or a visit. *Terrible*, he thought .

Less than an hour later she had her MRI. The results would be given to her after the radiologist read it and issued a report to Dr. Goldstein.

"I'm exhausted, Robert. Let's skip lunch and take me home," she instructed Robert.

He prepared a light meal for her and asked Stasha, who was cleaning that day, to be extra quiet since Mrs. Moore wasn't feeling well.

***

Less than a week later, Dr. Goldstein called. Robert answered the phone "Mrs. J.P. Moore's residence. Can I help you?"

"Yes, Robert. This is Doctor Goldstein. Is Mrs. Moore available to come to the phone?"

"Let me get her," Robert replied and within 30 seconds he brought the heavy push-button phone with a 50-foot line to her in the study where she was reclining.

"It's Doctor Goldstein. He wants to speak with you"

"This is Jackie, Dr. Goldstein. I assume that you have the results of the MRI?" she asked.

"Yes. Something is happening. The tumor actually seems to have shrunk albeit a bit but it has not expanded. It seems like your previous treatment has helped." Dr. Goldstein

32

went on to give her the measurements of the minimal decrease in centimeters which meant nothing to Mrs. Moore but she was obviously pleased with the results.

"Thank you, doctor. You are keeping this old gal alive longer than I expected," she said with a ring in her voice. "I think you and Robert are doing a good job."

With that she told Robert the news and he was elated. Robert gave her a sincere hug and asked if she would be up to a celebration dinner at Blue Bell.

"Call Bill Spaulding and ask if he and his wife will join us for a double celebration. You know, Robert it is one year now that you have been here" she informed Robert, who hadn't realized it had been that long, time went so quickly.

"I know that he will be excited also to hear the good news about your health," Robert responded and then called Bill Spaulding.

"Mrs. Moore and I would like to invite you and your wife to join us at Blue Bell Inn tonight to celebrate the good news concerning her tumor's regression," Robert joyfully requested. Even though Bill had some late work at his office he graciously accepted the offer. He had planned to have a meeting with her in a couple of weeks since it was time to update her will.

"Her usual 5:30 pm late dinner?" Which he used to joke about since his own dinners were usually at 8 pm or later.

"Yes, 5:30." Then Robert placed the phone back on its cradle.

Chapter 4

"I'd like to go to dinner in the gray Mercedes Gullwing, but I know that is impossible. I think the last time I was in that car was many years before I broke my hip. Even then I was able to get in then but getting out took all of my husband's strength helping me." She knew that it was not going to happen. It was just her way of reflecting back to when she was very mobile.

"My dear Mrs. Moore. Would you want me to take your Buick Limited again? Robert was referring to her two-year-old black Buick sedan with tan crushed velour seating that was extremely comfortable. "You know it's been used very seldom by me just doing local errands and your last trip to Dr. Goldstein's. When Victor is here and has time on his hands, I see to it that he keeps your car washed and waxed," Robert claimed.

"Good idea, Robert. No sense using the old Cadillac more than necessary," she acknowledged.

At 4:45 pm, after Mrs. Moore was seated and her wheelchair placed in the trunk, Robert headed to the Blue Bell. Arriving at 5:30 he leaned over to open the glove compartment and depress the trunk release button and was ready to take out her wheelchair when Mrs. Moore shouted,

"No, Robert! My cane is all that I want. I am feeling in a celebratory mood and I will not ruin it sitting in that monstrosity." She was adamant but in a good way.

They walked into the Blue Bell Inn and now Dorothy was checking coats in the cloakroom.

"Hello Mrs. Moore," Dorothy welcomed her with her deep German accent.

"Thirty years now?" Mrs. Moore inquired.

"Nope. Forty years, Mrs. Moore and I am going to retire next year," Dorothy replied as she took Mrs. Moore's full-length cashmere coat and Robert's trench coat to hang up. No coat check was necessary since Dorothy knew everyone that frequents her family's restaurant.

As they headed towards the bar on their right you could hear "Jackie, Great timing!" as Bill and his wife of twenty years arrived almost simultaneously. Neither wore any coats to be checked in and they followed Robert and Mrs. Moore. Robert was extra careful holding onto Mrs. Moore as she navigated down the one step into the bar.

After being seated the bartender prepared Mrs. Moore's favorite drink: a Kamikaze made with vodka, Rose's lime juice, and Cointreau for both she and Robert. Bill's wife asked for the same; however, Bill wanted straight Grey Goose chilled with an olive and a twist of lemon.

"Oosters, anyvone?" Dorothy requested if the guests would like Blue Bell's famous fried oysters given away at the bar. Without knowing her personally one would think that there are two or three Dorothy's working there. Hands reached out from every direction and within seconds a large platter of fried oysters disappeared.

"Please tell me, Jackie. The good news?" asked Bill.

"First I want to thank Robert for putting up with me for one year today. He made my past year a pleasure and quite a relief having him look after everything. Robert is a good friend and I will never forget his caring nature. Secondly, which may actually be tied to the first, is that the tumor on my brain has decreased in size, surprising the hell out of the doctor and without a doubt me also. For some strange reason since

Robert has taken on the task of looking after me and the estate everything is been going wonderful. So let's celebrate please all of us and I include you Bill because you recommended Robert." As Mrs. Moore raised her kamikaze the three others joined for a toast.

"Another round please, Thomas," Bill told the bartender who like Dorothy had been working there for 40 plus years.

Peering into the bar area the maître d' walked up to Mrs. Moore and told her that her table was ready as the busboy reached out to bring everyone's drinks to the dining room.

Mrs. Moore was giddy from having two Kamikaze's even though seldom did a day pass that she did not have some alcoholic beverage intake. Everyone had a menu but without looking at anything everyone knew exactly what they wanted to eat including Robert. From his many weekly trips to the Blue Bell Inn, he knew that he never had a sirloin strip taste as good as the chef made. On top of that, he covered it with Sauce Bearnaise another specialty of the Inn. Mrs. Moore ordered her calves liver and sautéed onions with slices of bacon and she also had two heaping tablespoons of the Sauce Bearnaise. Mrs. Spaulding, having only been there once before ordered the same thing that she had previously, rare prime ribs as did her husband Bill. Each portion was more than the average person with a good appetite could consume in one meal and many customers carried home doggy bags for themselves. On some occasions, their dogs actually had something to eat if they did not eat it themselves.

After the meal, everyone embraced each other stating how much they enjoyed the celebration and looked forward to doing it again.

Robert pulled the car up and escorted Mrs. Moore into the front seat of the Buick sedan and headed to Hampton Court.

Mrs. Moore was elated after the wonderful meal and the company of her attorney and his wife and Robert. By the time they arrived home, she was ready to go to sleep. Robert helped her to her bedroom and escorted himself out, making sure that the light remained on in the hallway.

He left the Buick outside and went up the second floor to his apartment and turned the television on. Within an hour Robert fell asleep also.

***

Two weeks had passed and Bill Spaulding's new secretary placed a call to Mrs. Moore reminding her that Bill had an appointment with her at her estate the following day at 2 p.m.

At 1:55 p.m. Bill telephoned from his car that he would be 15 minutes late since there was an accident on the interstate. When he arrived it wasn't necessary to use the remote gate opener as Mrs. Moore opened it from inside the house. Because of the private nature of their annual estate planning, Mrs. Moore had requested that Robert take off the rest of the afternoon rather than have discussions behind his back.

Robert complied and decided to take the Gullwing Mercedes out on the road for a good workout.

***

Bill Spaulding sat in the living room with her and started by asking Jackie if she would mind if he used a tape recorder so that he would have exact notes in order to update her estate. Mrs. Moore had no objections and even thought that was a good idea. Bill listened as Jackie told him once again how appreciative she was of Bill finding Robert for her. Bill had asked her if either of her nieces or nephews have contacted her only to find her tone turn from extremely pleasant to sounding upset.

"I cannot stand any of them. Not one of them. They only care about themselves and are so selfish it upsets me. Even when they were younger I saw that in them however, I felt that when they got older they would change. They never did." she said in anger.

"You do have them in your will," Bill said. "Do you want to reduce what you have left for them?"

"Bill, when you say reduce that means they would still get something. I don't want to leave them a damn cent. Please make sure that they are totally eliminated from anything."

Bill asked if she was going to leave the main portion of her estate to a foundation after finding out that one of the heads of the foundation recently made the newspapers. It was discovered that he was using the foundation's money for his lavish personal use and not to the charities that were supposed to receive it.

"Money does strange things to people," said Mrs. Moore.

"I agree and I have a suggestion for you. I see that we both made the right choice in picking Robert and I think that you should set aside a very meager amount for him," said Bill.

"Absolutely not! Leave Robert a meager amount? He's the only one that has cared about me. I think he has helped my mind and my body since I have not felt this good for such a long time. He is honest. He is loyal. He is a friend. I love him like the son that I never had. I want him to have everything," she said emphatically.

"It certainly is your decision and that's why I am here. I understand how you feel and would probably feel the same way myself." Bill smiled.

Chapter 5

About a month after Mrs. Moore received her upbeat health report, Robert tried to convince her to start once again with physical therapy. She resisted; however, he kept trying to persuade her even to the point that he said, "Let the therapist come once or twice and teach me how to give you the therapy. After that, you can then decide to continue or not."

"Robert. You are the sweetest, and I really do appreciate it and yes I will agree only because I have been feeling so much better and I stopped dwelling on death because of you," she said.

With that, Robert contacted her orthopedic surgeon to get a new prescription for physical and massage therapy and Mrs. Moore gave Robert the name of the last person that had taken care of her. A few days later he received the prescription and then contacted Lawrence, the therapist, who did not have an opening for Mrs. Moore for a period of two weeks.

"That is fine. Kindly put it down as being firm that you will be here two weeks from now on Tuesday at 11 a.m. I will have her ready for your treatment," Robert responded.

Two weeks to the day, Joanne visited Mrs. Moore bringing a duffel bag containing liniments and items to microwave that would apply heat to soften tight muscles. She spent over an hour gently stretching all of Mrs. Moore's muscles, concentrating on her glutes and hip socket. She explained each muscle and joint to both of them and instructed Robert how to continue until her next visit the following week. She handed Robert a brochure and circled the items that she wanted Robert to stress until she returned. Mrs. Moore had none of the objections that she had the year before because she felt so much more comfortable with Robert there. The following month she continued with Robert who she felt was doing a better job than Joanne, which may have been strictly mental. It made no difference since Mrs. Moore after two weeks was walking significantly better although she still used a cane.

As the spring and summer quickly passed and fall approached Mrs. Moore requested that Robert not use the Eldorado convertible nor their modern Buick sedan for their weekly trips to Blue Bell Inn and use her 'darling' Rolls Royce sedan which was her husband's car of choice for their dinner trips. Robert did not hesitate at all since she never had mentioned to him which car she preferred. It was his duty and his obligation to care for her; he wanted to do whatever made her feel good. He was so happy that she was progressing, even walking more upright than before and looking very stately.

***

One evening after arriving at Blue Bell Inn with the silver Rolls Royce sedan Mrs. Moore opened up the passenger's door herself before Robert had a chance to get there. Robert could not believe how quickly she exited the door and walked in front of the car heading to the walkway by herself. Robert was stunned.

"Mrs. Moore. Please wait for me; God forbid you might trip." Mrs. Moore obliged by standing there waiting for him to escort her in.

Everyone knew Mrs. Jacqueline Moore and now they all knew Robert Snyder as well. The piano player in the bar played her favorite tune, a Johnny Mathis song, "Misty." Robert pulled two chairs up to the piano while they both enjoyed their kamikazes. Mrs. Moore ordered a drink for Edward, the piano player. A friend of Mrs. Moore sent another round of drinks over for both of them. Robert wanted to turn it down since he was being more responsible than ever caring about her safety and well-being.

"Oh Robert!" she exclaimed. " Don't be such a fuddy-duddy."

Having consumed too many kamikazes, both of them were a little bit tipsy and after having their meals Robert was growing tired. He ordered a black coffee for both of them but she refused. As soon as they arrived back at Hampton Court Robert saw to it that she made it to her bedroom and he left the hall light on and retired to his carriage house apartment. He fell asleep immediately.

***

Early the following morning Stasha arrived to do her general house cleaning. Robert was still in bed with a slight hangover. Stasha went straight to the utility room to pick up a mop and a bucket to lightly clean the floors in the living room dining room and kitchen but got very concerned when she saw one table laying on its side and a broken lamp. Drawers were opened in the cupboard and the sideboard drawers were scattered on the floor. Sensing something had happened she knocked on Mrs. Moore's bedroom door but there was no response. She knocked again." Mrs. Moore are you all right?"

Stasha grabbed the door handle, opened the door and screamed. "Oh my God! Oh my God!" Stasha shook her but there was no life.

Mrs. Jacqueline Moore was motionless. Blood had oozed out of her forehead. She was dead. Stasha then started screaming and ran to Robert's apartment to tell him. She never moved so fast in her life running up the steps of the carriage house apartment. She hammered on the door with her hand, yelling "Mr. Robert Mr. Robert!" Robert opened the door to see Stasha panicking. She told him that Mrs. Moore

41

is dead. He left her there and ran full speed straight to the house.

Then opening up the front door his eyes moved right to left witnessing the disarray of furniture and items thrown around. Moments later Stasha was there still screaming. Then he saw her lying there with her head hanging over the side of the bed and a pool of blood on the floor. Robert panicked. His adrenaline was pumping. He started screaming "No, no, no, why? Dear God, why?" He was shaking never thinking for a moment that whoever did this may still be in the house. He ran to get the phone and called the police.

Within three minutes lights were flashing in patrol cars and an ambulance crew jumped out of the rear doors with emergency gear. It was to no avail since Mrs. Moore was dead.

One officer from Upper Kellington Police Department went into his patrol car and placed a call for a homicide detective and a fingerprint specialist. Moments later yellow tape was being stretched around the house as other officers arrived.

In the meantime Robert was pacing feverishly and mumbling, "It's my fault, it's my fault, it's my fault."

At the same time, Stasha was sitting in the club chair crying with her head bent over into her cupped hands. "No! No! No!"

Neighbors came over to see what all the excitement was about but the police told them to please leave the premises. A few newspaper reporters were at the front door trying to get in when the newly arrived Detective Theodore Harrison stopped them in their tracks. "Stand back behind the tape. This is a crime scene." His six-foot four-inch large-framed body spoke volumes. As he entered he shouted to everyone, "do not touch a thing."

Detective Harrison asked, "Which officer arrived here first?"

One police officer said "Aldrich" at which time Aldrich walked up to identify himself as the first officer on the scene.

"Paul, have you spoken with anyone here yet?" Detective Harrison asked.

"So far it seems as though there's just two people here. One a housekeeper or maid who just about speaks English and the other a young man who appears to be Mrs. Moore's administrator or property manager who lives in the carriage house next door."

"Any observations that I should know about?" asked the detective.

"Looks like somebody got in and was looking for something in particular to steal since drawers and cabinets were opened and items thrown all around," Aldrich responded. At the end of the hallway on the right is Mrs. Moore's bedroom. It looked like a small-caliber bullet to the forehead."

"Did anyone call to get this place dusted? " asked Detective Harrison.

"I did, and Howard is on his way," stated Aldrich.

Wanting to see the body first, Detective Harrison walked through to the end of the hall passing both Robert and Stasha.

"This had to be a 22-caliber because the back of her head is still intact," Detective Harrison mumbled to himself.

Within 15 minutes Howard was dusting the areas around the crime scene starting first in the bedroom. When that was finished he spent the next several hours going from room to room. During that time Detective Harrison interviewed Robert Snyder and Stasha individually and recorded his notes.

Detective Harrison questioned Stasha, who was not easy to interview. It seemed as though every question she would nod her head every time, when in reality she didn't understand half the questions. He was able to ascertain that she has no husband and lived with her boyfriend Aleksander. She had been in the country for nearly 20 years and is a naturalized citizen. She was at home with her boyfriend since 6 p.m. the previous day and did not leave to come to work until 7:30 this morning. He jotted down the information on her driver's license and Social Security card so he could further investigate and asked her to get him the same information on Aleksander.

At least it was easier questioning Robert Snyder once he was able to settle him down. Harrison felt that Robert really was in a traumatic state seeing him shake and tremble while he kept walking around in a state of shock constantly repeating, "it was my fault, it was my fault. I should've never have gone to sleep so early."

Robert told the detective that he had been working for Mrs. Moore for about a year and a half but the date he first started had slipped his mind. He was in charge of the estate. He was authorized to write checks and pay bills. He was to hire contractors and or laborers for whatever work he thought was necessary in order to keep the property in proper condition. He was to check on Mrs. Moore's health status and make certain that she ate properly and took all her medications on time. Detective Harrison asked Robert for the names of any other employees and recent contractors or subcontractors that had worked on or about the premises. Robert told the detective that besides the housekeeper there was only Victor who took care of the grounds. The detective wanted to know where he could find Victor and Robert looked through the address book on his desk and provided Victor's full information including his phone number. Robert was still visibly shaking when looking through the address book and the Detective took note of this.

"There were similar break-ins with violent deaths that occurred in this and surrounding areas over the past years," stated the detective. However, that did little to assuage Robert's emotional state.

"Mr. Snyder. Please tell me what work you have done prior to being the manager here at Hampton Court?" asked Harrison.

"Honestly, not much of anything. After graduating Temple University I entered law school but my desire to be a famous actor was more overwhelming than my desire to be a lawyer so after one year I dropped out of law school to be an actor. I took classes in drama I had small jobs here and there that my agent found for me. I took whatever parts that I could, even one time in a musical that failed during the first week. I loved that woman. She was like a mother to me and she treated me as if I was the son that she never had," Robert answered, nearly crying.

The detective also wrote down the information on Robert's driver's license and his Social Security card. He seemed to believe that Robert was very sincere but his background in acting made the detective's ears perk up.

While Robert was questioned, the medical examiner was photographing the corpse of Mrs. Jacqueline Moore. When he was done, the coroner and his aide placed the body on a gurney, covered it, and wheeled it out of the house to be placed in the back of the van and then taken to the morgue for further examination.

Detective Harrison instructed the housekeeper and Robert not to touch anything, hoping that Stasha understood. To be emphatic, he told her once again. To no avail, she nodded her head in agreement.

The detective asked if Victor the groundskeeper was on the property the day before.

"I didn't see him, Robert replied. "All the grounds are in order and not in need of attention. I assume that he will be here within the next day or so since he also has other people locally that he does work for but mainly here at Hampton Court."

"Mr. Snyder. Who has keys to enter the main house?" questioned Detective Harrison. "Since nowhere do we find any sign of forcible entry."

After Robert settled down somewhat, he remembered that Mrs. Moore lost a set of her keys weeks before. He was going to have all the locks changed but she refused saying that, "They will show up. I've lost them many times before and found them a day or two later."

"Several months ago she lost them when the therapist was here but subsequently found them about a week later."

45

"That's not uncommon," stated Detective Harrison. "At her age, people are lucky if they remember who they are. What I need to know is who else had keys to this house."

"Stasha has a set of keys for all the buildings, Victor also has a set of keys just as I do. I don't know of anyone else that does."

"That's it?" asked Detective Harrison.

"No one else at all, detective, that I know of. Well, there's her attorney."

Chapter 6

By 6 p.m. that evening, the house of been cleared of the fingerprint specialist, several police officers, the medical examiner and Detective Harrison. Robert looked around the interior of the house and felt a terrible void. He kept blaming himself but one part of his brain knew that he did nothing wrong. He went to the carriage house apartment, opened the bottle of vodka dropped in a few ice cubes and sat there sipping it feeling so sad. He did not feel this way when his own mother passed away. There was something special the way he cared for her and her kindness towards him.

He took the list Jacqueline Moore's relatives from her personal directory and was about to call her nieces and nephews when he realized he forgot to call Bill Spaulding. Bill had already left the office so Robert called him on his car phone. Moments later Bill picked up the phone and Robert started to cry. "She's gone. Mrs. Moore was murdered last night. I can't believe this. I don't know what to do. I've never been in a position like this in my life." Robert kept rattling on as his nerves were getting to him.

"What? What the hell are you talking about? Jackie is dead? She has been murdered?" Bill yelled into the phone. You could hear how upset and shocked he was.

"I'm sorry I didn't call you earlier, honestly. It has been pure mayhem. I've been questioned by everybody and I'm still shaking knowing that she's not here anymore. Somebody came in and killed her either late last night after we came back from dinner or very early this morning. The police detective said that she was shot in the head with a 22-caliber bullet. "

"This is horrible," said Bill. "I can't believe it happened. If anything, the way she seemed when we all were at dinner for your first anniversary working for her she seemed like she could live forever. Then when I met with her months ago to update her will she seemed so happy between her medical results and your help"... He stopped as if he was gasping for breath. "I'm going to have to come over and go over funeral arrangements. Where is her body?"

"The coroner took it," replied Robert. "I was just going to call her nephews and nieces when I realized that I hadn't called you. Please forgive me that I didn't call you first thing."

Robert didn't even realize that less than a minute or two before he had told Bill the same thing. Bill must realize that Robert's nerves were shot.

"I'm not going to go to the office tomorrow morning. I'm going to come straight to you. See you at 8:30?" Bill asked.

"Yes." Robert hung up the phone and sipped the vodka even though the ice cubes were almost melted. He went on to call both nieces and both nephews. They were the only living relatives that Mrs. Moore had. He told them that he would get back to them when he knew what the funeral arrangements were going to be. None of them seemed to care.

***

The following morning promptly at 8:30 Bill Spaulding pulled up in his black Mercedes sedan reached into the telephone box and then decided not to call ahead being that Mrs. Moore was dead. He used his remote gate opener and drove to the parking area in front of the carriage house. Mrs. Moore's black Buick sedan that Robert had used for errands

48

was outside. He looked up to the carriage house to see if a light was on thinking that he might have to wake up Robert when he heard—

"Bill. Thank God you're here." Robert had just opened up the front door of the carriage house apartment and started to walk towards Bill. As soon as they were face-to-face Robert put his arms around Bill hugging him and then he started to cry once again repeating. "If I had not gone to bed so early, this may never have happened."

Bill tried to comfort Robert, patting him on the back and hugging him. "This is terrible. Who in the world would do such a thing? What is here that's worth anything? Her paintings? Nobody would try to steal the paintings, they're too traceable."

They went into the house, finding that Stasha had already been straightening up the since she returned at 6:30 in the morning much earlier than she ever had before. Stasha told them she couldn't sleep at all after such a terrible day.

Bill Spaulding and Robert walked around the house not saying anything to each other and after less than a minute, Bill said to Robert. "How about we get out of this house and go to your apartment? I have three different funeral homes that we could use. Do you have any preference?" He showed Robert a list of names, none of which meant anything to him, as they exited the main house.

Once upstairs, Robert said, "Call whoever you want, Bill. I have no preference. I've never had anything like this experience before in my life."

Bill then dialed using Robert's phone.

Bill Spaulding took charge which was a relief for Robert. He made arrangements for the funeral home to pick up the body of Mrs. Jacqueline P. Moore and coordinated it with the coroner's office after the medical examiner was through with the corpse. The funeral home had asked for any pertinent information that may be interesting about Mrs. Jacqueline P. Moore's background most of which was filled in and completed by Bill Spaulding, who had known her for many years with a few sentences of love and admiration inserted by Robert. A newspaper listing was placed in the Philadelphia Inquirer's late-night edition in the obituary column and ran an extra day.

Robert then went through Mrs. Moore's personal directory again, this time trying to discern any friends that she had but since he found no notations it was difficult. He spent a couple of hours on the phone contacting person after person on the list hoping that he would find a dear friend, a previous college classmate or people who knew her and would like to attend the funeral service. To his dismay, the people that she had mentioned during his time with her were either deceased or in poor health. Only a few said they would do their best to attend.

As it turned out, the funeral attendance was sparse. There was Victor the groundskeeper, Stasha the house cleaner, and about a half a dozen neighbors. Two were former friends, however, not ones that were in touch. One was a frail 85-year-old frail whose husband had been a dear golfer friend of Jaqueline's deceased husband. Robert, of course, along with Bill Spaulding, his wife and both their children were there. The service did not last 30 minutes and everyone seemed to disperse in different directions. Robert did not want to have anyone over to the house for he was in mourning.

***

Two days later Bill called Robert to tell him to be at his office the following Monday for the reading of the will.

"This should be short and sweet Robert, since you are the only beneficiary, see buddy. It's a shame that things turned out the way that they did. I liked the old fart myself," he said.

Robert was furious. "Do not ever refer to her like that," he commanded.

Chapter 7

The following Monday Robert appeared at the offices of Calhoun, Spaulding, and Fiengold, as directed. He went directly to Bill Spaulding's office where Bill's secretary was expecting him and nodded as Robert walked in for his meeting. They shook hands and patted each other on the back in a comforting manner.

"Well, this is actually going to be easier than I thought it would be. I posted the proper notices in newspapers about her demise and received no responses with the exception of a few advertisements. Robert, you are the sole beneficiary of her entire estate. It seems as though I never had to convince her she wanted you to be the recipient. She really loved you as a son and a confidant," Bill said.

Robert, still affected by the shock of her death, replied, "I cared so much about her. I miss her I don't know what to do without her."

"Well, you won't have to worry about money. The home alone is worth nearly $2 million in a good market; however, with the real estate market the way it is, I don't know how long it will take to come up with offers or even a sale. Some of the real estate agents that I've used have informed me that there are homes in this area that have been on the market for over six months without one offer," Bill stated.

Bill continued, "I can suggest a couple of agents for you, if you would like, even though I am the executor for the estate. I'd be glad to take your suggestions. From what I see you could stay there but, knowing you, where would you receive the income to pay the bills? What's left in cash and CDs won't last too long. She lived off her annuities, which were substantial as you know, since you recorded her income and paid the bills. But after death, Social Security and all annuities cease. Besides, dear friend you remember our agreement, I am sure, you owe me one-third of the value now."

Robert really could not have cared less. He was still in a semi-state of shock with the passing of his dear friend. He asked Bill, "What do you suggest?"

***

The real estate broker arrived a few days later to look at the interior and take notes. A day after that someone installed a sign: 'Hampton Court for Sale' with the broker's name and telephone number. It was up no more than two days when the broker called that he had an interested buyer. Robert permitted the broker to show the main house and the outbuildings, including the carriage house, while he drove into town to get a sandwich and coffee.

He stayed as long as he could and then drove back. The broker and the young couple were gone; Robert was glad. He did not know how to handle his mixed emotions. Now this is his property and he loved it but certainly could not afford to keep it.

The broker called Robert the following day to say that the couple turned out to be investors that were as she called it 'bottom fishing,' meaning they were quick to purchase—if the price was cheap enough—for them to make a profit when the market hopefully would turn around. He expressed the difficulty in selling a property when there were few buyers, if any, especially in the price range close to two million dollars.

"We are currently even having a difficult time selling houses in developments that are priced at two hundred thousand," the broker commented. "Unless you are willing to give it away, be prepared to hold onto it for some time."

***

The next day Bill Spaulding called. "Robert, how do you intend to pay me my one third per our agreement?"

Robert was shocked. "How can I pay you anything when I don't have more than the savings in my account since I have worked here?"

"Sell the home. Everything cleared probate so it is yours and uncontested. According to our agreement, that means you owe me the money now. It stated within 30 days. I am sending you a notice of demand. I'm only doing it as a formality. Hopefully, you will find a buyer quickly. Just remember that the clock is running."

Robert called the broker and asked if anyone had replied from their small display advertisement in the Philadelphia Inquirer. "None," the broker told him. "According to real estate practices I am required to present any offers no matter what the price may be and I have only one. I am reluctant to present it because it is so low and the property has just been listed."

"Well. What is their offer?" Robert asked and was shocked when the broker replied. "$750,000 with everything in it as it was shown. That means they want an inventory but they will close as soon as they get a clear title search."

"That is insane. I don't know real estate values but that just cannot be," Robert painfully continued. "Over a year ago the neighbor down the street sold their property for over one million and that was a piece of junk that was in disrepair. Besides, the cars were promised to someone else and cannot be part of any sale so forget about it."

"Mr. Snyder, I realize how traumatic something like this is. I am just reporting as I am required to do. I am certain that the buyer would still go through with the offer without the cars however I would have to verify that. In the meantime let's hope that I can find some interested potential buyers. Just be patient."

Robert could not afford to be patient. He called Bill the following morning after preparing his coffee. "That son of a bitch agent brought some thief here to buy the property with everything, including the cars, and made an offer that is ridiculous." Robert's voice was extremely elevated.

"Slow down, Robert. It sounds like you have consumed too much caffeine," responded Bill. "You know that this is the wrong time to sell real estate. Things are simply not selling. At least you say that you have an offer. Am I correct?"

"The real estate broker said that he had an offer for $750,000 and that included all the furnishings and the automobiles. The potential buyer was a relative of a neighbor who knew the property. Supposedly he would settle immediately," replied Robert.

"Well, look at it this way. If you cannot get more from the buyer and there are no other buyers, then $750,000 may be too cheap to sell it for, but what else can you do? I'd rather you get 2 million for it since I would get 1/3 of that. Tell me Robert, would you want to have nearly $500,000 in cash? You know that you could live a good life with that!" Bill continued, "I really would love to see you get $2 million and if it wasn't that I made a very bad investment need the money, I would want you to wait until the market changes, whether it's in a year or two years or more, but I cannot wait."

With that, the proverbial ball was in Robert's court.

"Robert, do yourself a favor and call the broker to see if they will buy it without the cars and then grab it," Bill strongly suggested.

This was something that was totally out of Robert's comprehension. Here he has to make a quick decision to sell or keep it and not be able to pay the bills. He could not afford to hold on. $750,000 was beyond any amount of money he could have ever dreamed about. Even after giving one third to Bill for everything that he had done for him in the past. Robert felt that Bill deserved it since it was his help that got him the job of a lifetime. Before Robert questioned himself any more he found himself calling the broker. "If they will make the deal without the cars then I will agree," he told Seth the agent handling it.

"I will let the broker know. I am hopeful that you will have a deal but one never knows anything for certain dealing with real estate," Seth informed Robert.

***

The following day Robert received a phone call from agent Seth informing him that the buyer's representative presented a $50,000 deposit with settlement to be held within 30 days or less without any conditions except clear title. Before Robert would sign anything though he needed his attorney to take a look at the papers. The agent agreed to bring it to Bill Spaulding's office first for his approval.

"Robert, it looks like you have yourself a deal. Congratulations," said Bill upon reviewing the contract of sale.

***

Less than three weeks later on December 19th settlement took place at Calhoun, Spaulding, and Fiengold. The sale price was $750,000.From that total the settlement sheet showed title transfer fees, real estate taxes, deed preparation fees, attorney fees, and special loan advancement due William Spaulding of $250,000. Then the Pennsylvania Inheritance Tax of $112,500 was subtracted which was 15% for non-related inheritance recipients. The title company clerk issued Robert the check in the amount of $332,500 and he was excited, temporarily forgetting that he was the beneficiary of Mrs. Moore's death.

Before leaving the settlement office Bill had Robert come into his private office and sign the titles over to him. Bill told Robert, "My gift to you is this the title to the Buick sedan since I don't want you to have to use that money to buy a new car."

Robert thanked him for everything.

Chapter 8

Robert now had to be prudent with his newfound wealth since he was without a job and needed a place to live. Neither presented a problem at this time because there were many apartments available in close proximity to Center City without the high rents of the city. He had asked at settlement if could he stay another week but that was rejected. Bill Spaulding told him that it would be impossible because of liability and that they would have to construct a lease to protect the new owner for a week. Bill had given Robert the names of a few of his clients that owned residential apartment buildings for him to inspect. He even went as far as suggesting that he could come and stay at his house until he found a place to live permanently but Robert did not want to impose on Bill and his family and thanked him for the offer.

He drove the perimeter of the city from South Philadelphia to the Fairmount section finding and inspecting three furnished apartment units to choose from the list that Bill had recommended. He settled on second a floor apartment with the rental of $750 a month plus utilities on Fairmount Avenue.

Writing out a check for $2250.00 to the real estate agent later that afternoon was something he could not have done two years ago without his check bouncing.

Robert had to have all his belongings removed from the Hampton Court by noon the next day. Robert's head was spinning. He had butterflies in his stomach all day. The woman that he cared about was murdered. Then he had to sell everything, rushing in every direction so quickly. Now, he just found a place to stay and signed a lease but he had left everything at Hampton Court, including his old junker that he occasionally started to keep the battery up.

He was barely able to sleep in his new surroundings, especially since this bed was not as comfortable as the one that he had slept on for nearly two years. Robert washed up and went out to get breakfast at a local sandwich shop. By 8 a.m. he took his Buick sedan and headed back for his last visit to Hampton Court in Gladwyne.

When he arrived it was not quite 9 o'clock. He used the remote and opened the gate and went straight to his apartment to remove all his clothing and odds and ends. He filled up his trunk and had a full suit bag lying on the rear seat. He did not go in the house, fearing that he would see images of Mrs. Moore when she was killed, even though the images that floated in and out of his mind were beyond his control.

The phone in the Buick's console was still activated and Robert wanted to know if anything was happening in the investigation. He took Detective Harrison's card out of his wallet and placed a call to him.

"Harrison," the detective answered.

"Detective Harrison, this is Robert Snyder. I'm just calling to find out how you are progressing. Can you tell me anything?"

"We're still checking out leads. We have a few things that we're working on however I really cannot reveal anything to you," claimed Detective Harrison.

"I'm not going to be at Hampton Court anymore since I sold it. I just signed a lease for an apartment in Philadelphia,

Robert informed the detective. "If you want, I can call you when I get a telephone line installed."

"Mr. Snyder. I'm a bit confused. If I heard you correctly you said that you just sold Hampton Court?"

"Yes, Mrs. Moore left her estate to me, which was quite a surprise and I certainly can't afford to keep it, so I took the first offer that was received. I'm looking for a job now so if you know anyone, I'd appreciate it if you could pass the number to me."

Detective Harrison just had a jolt when Robert told him that he was the sole beneficiary of Mrs. Moore's estate. *What a motive,* he thought

***

After a couple of weeks Robert was feeling comfortable in his apartment. He now had a phone line and an answering machine hooked up. Robert left a message for Detective Harrison leaving him his address and his new telephone number. He contacted a newly formed organization that he read about in the newspapers called "Wheelz2Work" and made arrangements for them to inspect his Oldsmobile sedan so that he could donate it to a needy person or family. He told them the car does not look great but it does run well and it's dependable. Two days later they picked up the automobile and he gave them the title.

Robert followed every employment advertisement that he saw, hoping to get some kind of job. He realized that he had no career in acting but still sent out feelers when he heard about any auditions that may be available. He called a couple of neighbors asking if they knew of anyone who could use a property manager with no results.

His bank account was huge but he felt uncomfortable using the money to pay his bills; however, he had no choice not having found a job that he would qualify for. His days were becoming monotonous and very boring. He wanted to do something. He'd take almost any kind of job if it was offered.

Browsing that Sunday's paper he saw the advertisement for the Grand Philadelphia Antique and

Classic auto show that was taking place that day alongside the art museum in Fairmount Park.

Chapter 9

As Amanda kept showing him various pieces of artwork in her beautiful penthouse, Robert didn't know how to tell her that for close to two years he had been living in the lap of luxury. He was waiting for her to ask him what he's been doing with himself fearing that he may appear to be a gigolo in her eyes.

"I'm soaked throughout. How about you?" she asked.

"No problem; I'm fine thanks," he responded.

"Give me a minute while I make a quick change," she said as she headed into her bedroom.

Five minutes later she came out looking more gorgeous and sexier than she did when they both went to Temple. She had a beautiful classic look with her hair in a French braid and wearing a black lace dress with a deep the cut V-neck and a gold braided necklace. All this on a beautiful 5'5" slender build.

"Mandy. Honestly, you look more beautiful now than you did back at school and you were really a turn on." Robert could not hold back telling her and she was embarrassed or at least appeared to be. She opened up a bottle of 1977 Chardonnay by Burgess Vineyards as Mandy enthusiastically described to him what it's like being an assistant district attorney then she abruptly stopped and asked Robert," Florida pompano or sirloin strip? Your choice."

Robert stopped to gather his thoughts. "Whichever you prefer. What's pompano?"

"The best fish that you'll ever eat in your life. Not only that but I can prepare it and have it ready in ten minutes. When they are running, a fish purveyor in Vero Beach calls me and then I have them FedEx'd. These came in this morning."

She took out two fillets from the refrigerator and rubbed them with olive oil and then she placed them on an aluminum foil pan with the skin side up under the broiler. Less than ten minutes later the skin was crisp and blistery and Robert admitted that he never tasted anything so good. While that was in the boiler she blanched some string beans and carrots.

Sitting down at the dining room table and enjoying their meal together everything seemed so tranquil and lovely.

Then the bombshell question came.

"Robert, you sat here listening to me for about a half - hour or more as I've gone into every detail about my work and I rattled off so much I never asked you to bring me up to date with all your adventures these past years. Please tell me."

Robert felt it was time to lay it all out there. He told her that while he was in law school the urge to be an actor was overwhelming and he never went back for his second year. He explained that for years he had small bits in local theaters seldom making enough money to get by. If he wasn't being a waiter one night he'd be a bartender somewhere else and constantly kept dreaming about fame on Broadway which was never to be. Then he explained that he received a call from his agent and lawyer friend who claimed that he had a position for Robert.

"At first I was so excited I couldn't wait to get to his office. That was about two years ago. It turned out it was not an acting job that he had for me in the theater which disappointed me but the reality was I could barely make ends meet and was hanging out at different places and I needed a steady job. Before Robert could continue Amanda asked, "What was the job?"

Robert continued telling her that it was a position managing an estate for an elderly woman who was widowed with no children. She was ill and needed someone to look over her property with several buildings and beautiful gardens. He was also to write checks for her, pay bills and hire contractors or subcontractors for any work that may be needed. He was given his own carriage house apartment and the use of a car. As he told her these things he was embarrassed and he told her that he was embarrassed.

"I have no idea where I would be now had I not married Clarkson. You had a dream to be a great actor, but Robert you were always a great person with character and caring. That means more than wealth." She tried to comfort him then he continued.

"Several months back someone came into the house after we both returned from a dinner at Blue Bell Inn and had too many kamikazes. I fell asleep early after seeing that she had taken all her medications and was tucked in and first thing in the morning I heard the housekeeper screaming as I was walking towards the main house." Robert got choked up and continued, "Whoever it was shot her in the head killing her. The house was all the disheveled; however, it did not look that anything was really missing. The police came and I was hysterical because I grew so fond of her. She was like a mother and better than the mother that I had."

"Oh, I'm so sorry to hear that, Robert. That must've been terrible. I know working in the district attorney's office we see homicides every day and it affects so many people. Did they ever find the assailant?"

"I've called the detective several times over the past couple of months and he keeps telling me he's following leads and could not provide any information," Robert explained.

"Where did it happen? I mean the area—the township?" sounding like an investigator.

"In Gladwyne, Upper Kellington Township." He left out that he was the sole beneficiary and also that the lawyer took one-third of the estate.

Before long the bottle of Chardonnay was finished and as she went to open up a second bottle when Robert put his hand on hers and said," No. I don't want to have anything else to drink. Just talking to you feels good. "

The evening was a great relief for Robert. It was wonderful being in Amanda's company and reminiscing of old times. It was also great for Amanda for she felt a personal warmth with Robert there. They sat back on the sofa together listening to Johnny Mathis's songs until they looked into each other's eyes, embraced and kissed.

The following morning Amanda had coffee perking for Robert and she was off to work at City Hall leaving Robert to sleep. Upon awakening, he realized that Amanda had left and could smell the aroma of Arabica coffee permeating the penthouse. Robert poured a cup and sipped his coffee while reading the newspaper and taking his time for the appointment with his accountant that wasn't until 10 a.m.

Chapter 10

Walking into the offices of Boyle, Boyle, and Bernstein for his 10 o'clock appointment Robert was asked by the receptionist if he would like a 'cuppa kafee' since Mr. Boyle, not naming which one, would be finishing his meeting momentarily.

"Thank you. No. I've already had my cup of Java for the day."

He sat reading one of the magazines in the waiting room.

***

On the other side of town in City Hall, assistant district attorney Amanda Dillington placed a call to the Upper Kellington Township police requesting to speak with the detective covering the murder of Mrs. Jacqueline Phyllis Moore. She waited patiently while the operator tried to track down who was handling that case.

"From what I see Detective Harrison is the one handling that homicide. Can he call you back in ten minutes since he's finishing a meeting?" the receptionist asked Amanda.

"Please. Ask him to call me as soon as he has time." Amanda left her direct line with the receptionist.

Five minutes later Amanda's desk phone rang. It was Detective Harrison.

"What brings Philadelphia District Attorney's Office into this?"

"Hi, detective. This is Amanda Dillington. An old acquaintance of mine informed me of the tragic murder of Mrs. Moore. I just wanted to know if you could bring me up to date. According to him that he has been calling you almost weekly asking for information but has been turned down each time. "

"Your friend is Robert Snyder? He's the only one that's been calling me. No one else."

"Yes. It is Robert Snyder and he told me of his relationship with Mrs. Moore and how tragic it was and still is for him."

She confirmed.

"Did the son of a bitch tell you he's the sole benefactor of everything?"

Amanda was speechless. There was a significant hesitation before she replied. "Detective Harrison, I hope there's been progress over these past several months. Is there anything that you can share with me on a purely professional level that, I can assure you, will not go back to anyone."

"So far we have found that there was no break-in. Whoever killed her was someone who had access to her house. We have not found any fingerprints different than those that were usually in the house or about the house. At this point, Robert Snyder seems to have the only motive."

Amanda asked, "Why would he call you on a continual basis to see if you are progressing?"

"To cloud the issue!" The Detective answered.

"How about other people that you say had access to the house? Have you checked them out?"

"I have," the detective replied, "and each had an alibi."

Amanda was torn between her seriously wanting to believe in Robert and her instincts as an assistant district attorney.

***

Robert wished that he had never met with his accountant after going over his financial obligations to pay both the IRS and the State of Pennsylvania. Everything that he was just made aware of meant less and less money for him to the point that he would be in the same financial position as he was two years ago. His obligations, if delayed any longer, would mean penalties. Had he contacted an accountant for a recommendation prior to settlement the minimal advice would have been to postpone settlement until after the first of the year. That alone would have meant that his obligation to pay any taxes to the IRS would not happen until the following year. All accountants believe postpone, postpone. The accountant had requested that Robert bring his last few tax returns so that he could do everything if possible to somehow reduce his tax burdens.

Robert then realized that they were in his duffel bag that he had inadvertently left at Hampton Court the day that he removed his clothes and personal items from his apartment. But months have now passed and he had hoped that no one threw the bag in the trash believing it was unwanted.

Robert called Bill Spaulding's office to ask for the phone number of the new owners when the secretary told him that Bill was not there.

"Do you know where he is?" Robert asked.

The secretary informed him that he was on his way to his car collection in South Philly driving one of his new old cars. Robert knew that Bill kept a few cars in a building that he owned around Fitzwater Street and asked the secretary for the exact address since he wouldn't be able to be reached on his car phone if he was driving one of his old cars.

Minutes later, Robert was on the way to Bill Spaulding's garage. Once he arrived at the garage he was surprised to see that it wasn't a four or six-car garage but a

66

very large building that at one time housed a soda bottling company that had since gone out of business. He knocked on the door and a young man opened it   moments later. He informed the young man that he was not only a client of Bill Spaulding's but a dear friend.

"Come on in. Follow me."

To Robert's amazement he saw at least 75 automobiles, possibly more, lined up like soldiers and each with a sparkling finish. The interior was set up as a museum with gas pumps from the 30s, 40s, and 50s of all models and descriptions and signs from automotive dealerships that had gone out of business plus numerous mannequins dressed in uniforms that gas stations had for their employees during the same periods.

Robert saw the 65 Rolls Royce Silver Cloud 111, the 1956 Mercedes 300 SL Gullwing even the 1932 Cord four-door convertible but did not notice the 54 Eldorado convertible, which was his favorite car to drive

"Where's Bill?" he asked the attendant. The young man asked one of the other employees who was polishing a 1937 Cord Phaeton who told him that he went to lunch driving a 1953 Corvette.

"Does anyone know where Bill has the '54 Eldorado convertible?" Robert asked aloud so that anyone could hear.

From under the hood of one of the automobiles, he heard a voice yell back. "Yeah. He keeps it out at his home."

He thanked the young man and told him to ask Bill to give him a call when he has a chance. He left closing the door behind him.

He then headed towards Hampton Court hoping that his duffel bag would still be leaning against the wall in the garage where he placed that the first day that moved in.

He pulled up to the entranceway and not knowing the new owners he reached for the telephone intercom box in the stone pier which was hooked up to the main house. Several times he could hear the ring but no one picked up. He was ready to leave a note in the mailbox requesting that someone call him about his duffel bag when he reached into the glove compartment of his car to take a chance to see if the gate opener worked. Like magic it did. The gate opened. He pulled up to the carriage house garage and tried the opener for that and it also opened. Obviously, the new owners didn't feel it was necessary to go to the trouble of having a service person change the codes. The garage doors opened and Robert became instantly and totally confused. There was the 1954 Cadillac Eldorado convertible. But why in the world was the '54 El Dorado there when his guys in the shop told him that Bill had the car at his house? Sure enough behind the left rear of the Cadillac leaning against the wall was his duffel bag exactly where he left it the first day that he moved into Hampton Court. He picked it up and closed the doors behind him then exited the premises still in a quandary.

Robert was getting visibly upset. Did his friend and lawyer lie to him? Why was the '54 Cadillac Eldorado in the garage when his employees said that it was parked at Bill Spaulding's house? He thought that the best thing would be to confront Bill Spaulding.

Chapter 11

After receiving a call from the assistant district attorney Amanda Dillington, Detective Harrison started looking through his file which was sitting beneath a half a dozen other current cases. He realized that they had little or nothing to go on, nor any evidence and he had more pressing things, therefore he had been neglecting the murder investigation of Mrs. Moore. If he had been more thorough he realized that he would've picked up the information that Mrs. Moore left her entire estate to Robert Snyder and not Robert Snyder voluntarily telling him about it when he never asked.

He then found the information regarding Victor, the groundskeeper, and called some of the other neighbors he worked for trying to locate him. After three calls one neighbor Ted Johnson who lived in a small estate on the same road confirmed that Victor was there. Harrison asked Mr. Johnson to please tell Victor to remain there that he was on the way over.

In this file was also information regarding William Spaulding, the attorney who had an alibi as to where he was that entire evening. Harrison had placed a call to his house a couple of days after the murder took place and spoke to a woman who said she was Mrs. Spaulding and she verified that he was there from early that evening until he went to work the next day.

He was too frustrated trying to get through and make sense of the housekeeper, Stasha, and really never followed up with anything regarding her. He never realized that Stasha was supposed to get the information about Aleksander, her boyfriend. Then there was the physical therapist, Joanne, who he had only spoken to on the phone just one time. Since Mrs. Moore had lost her keys did the physical therapist take them and possibly give them to someone to rob the house? Could Victor have come back into the house using the key that he had or give it to someone? Did the housekeeper pick up the key and pretend that she was hysterical seeing the dead body? He was hoping that he could put this together one way or another without any interference from the Philadelphia District Attorney's Office. He was recently criticized one time by his peers for being lax in following up important cases and he didn't want this one to bite him in the backside when his retirement was less than one a year away.

Harrison got into his black unmarked sedan and headed to meet Victor. As he was nearing the neighbor's house, he passed Hampton Court on his right. In another quarter mile or so was the property where Victor was working. He saw someone on a Kubota tractor with a frontend loader pulling a tag-along trailer. His first thought was *That must be Victor.*

The young man was wearing headphones. Harrison tooted his horn three times quickly to get his attention, but no luck. He did it again leaning on the horn a little harder and that definitely worked. The young man turned around. It was in fact the young man that he interviewed at Hampton Court.

When Victor walked over to the detective's sedan, Harrison reached out to shake his hand.

"Victor. There were some things in my report that Detective Simpson noted in his follow up that need to be answered. The first concern is that when we did a background check on you it seems that you have four different addresses in the past two years none of which matches your driver's license nor your Social Security card information. Please explain this. "

With a Spanish accent, Victor tried to explain and opened his wallet to show Detective Harrison that he has a new address pointing out to the address he had written on a business card from a real estate agent. Then Victor explained that the places that he lived had multiple families sharing one apartment and he rented a room for himself from one of them.

"They no stay there long. They get better job and go somewhere else. So I find new place myself," he tried to explain. "I now live here. I want my own place with no other peoples." He showed the business card once again.

Victor then reached into his back pocket and unfolded a two-page apartment rental lease agreement in his own name. The Detective looked over the lease and noticed something a little unusual. For security deposit, it showed one-year rental paid in full in advance.$6000. He wondered where did this laborer get $6000 to pay one year in advance?

He then asked Victor for the name of the previous landlord where he lived; however, he did not know since he paid his rent for the room to the person that leased it. Without success, Harrison was ready to leave when he said, "Victor, tell me about your arrest two years ago."

"I no arrested. Never. Maybe you got some other Victor?"

Harrison wondered if that may be the case and said his goodbyes telling Victor to call his office no later than two weeks from today leaving him his business card.

Next to find Joanne. She had made just two physical therapy visits to Mrs. Moore at the same time Mrs. Moore was aware that her keys had disappeared. When he returned to the office he had Detective Harold Simpson bring him the folder with whatever information he found on the therapist, Joanne Lawrence. Detective Harrison was embarrassed to see how thin the file was. It was basically her name, address, telephone number, and a synopsis of the conversation that Simpson had with her.

It read as follows: "Contacted Joanne Lawrence who said that she was home with a friend and had only visited Mrs. Moore on two occasions. She denied ever taking the house keys and was sorry to hear that she had been murdered."

"That's it?" Harrison looked at Simpson with a pissed off expression on his face. "It looks like you spent two minutes on this.\Find out where she is. And do it now. Top priority!" demanded Harrison.

Detective Harrison knew that everybody dropped the ball here including himself. He could see why people around him we're getting upset that he just was looking at the clock for retirement and wasn't doing the excellent work for which he had been known for close to twenty years.

He presented a copy of the file to a young rookie. "Run a background check on this and make sure it's totally thorough. Also if there's any other names that pop-up as being associated with them, do background checks on them."

Harrison looked at all everyone who was there or had access pinning a 3x5 index card with each name to his bulletin board.

Less than 30 minutes later the rookie detective gave Harrison a file that was larger than the entire file covering everyone in or around the investigation.

"I'd like to put my foot up Simpson's ass. What kind of detective worth his salt would not have done a complete criminal background check on her? I don't see a background check on anyone." Harrison was frustrated that he let all this slip by under his watch. He was yelling out loud to himself.

From the records he was looking at, it was clear that Joanne Lawrence not only could have 'dirty hands' but that she was arrested twice during a drug bust investigation, although she was subsequently released. Her arrest occurred when she was living with a known drug dealer, Chaz Galloni. He was previously arrested multiple times; however, each time witnesses changed their story.

"That's Simpson. That dumb piece of shit! How in the world could he have not checked this out?" A totally frustrated Harrison was talking to himself once again.

"Simpson. Simpson. Get your ass in here now!" yelled Harrison and Detective Harold Simpson came running from his desk 50 feet away.

"If I wasn't here for close to 20 years I could see how my superiors, after looking at such a piece of crap follow up on a homicide, would want to throw me out. Tell me why I shouldn't report you?" Harrison questioned.

"Teddy. I went over this with you a few months ago and you were upset about something personal and told me just to finish it up and go home," Detective Simpson stated. "I just did what you told me to do. Tell me what you want me to do."

"Bring her in here as soon as you can. We've got plenty of questions for her," instructed Detective Theodore Harrison.

Simpson picked up the file and brought it over to his desk. He placed a call to her which was not answered. He left a message on the answering machine. "Miss Lawrence. This is Detective Harold Simpson. I need just a minute of your time to clear up some confusion regarding the ongoing investigation of Mrs. Jacqueline Phyllis Moore. Please call me as soon as possible. Thank you." Simpson hung up.

Chapter 12

"Good afternoon. This is Robert Snyder calling for William Spaulding."

"He will be with you in a moment, Mr. Snyder," the congenial secretary informed Robert.

"Hi, Robert. What's going on in your fascinating new life?" inquired Spaulding.

"Bill. I'm really confused. I went to look for you since your secretary thought that you were at your shop where you have your old cars stored. One of your employees told me that I just missed you, that you just took a 1953 Corvette out for a test drive and lunch. I was amazed seeing all the gorgeous and rare automobiles that you have there. Here I thought that you told me that you had four or five car.... Anyway, I saw the '65 Rolls Royce, the '32 Cord, and the '56 Gullwing Mercedes but I didn't see the '54 Eldorado. One of the guys yelled from under the hood of a car that it was at your house," Robert rattled off.

"So?" Bill asked.

"So, I went to an accountant's office that had been recommended to me to go over my tax returns for this year and was shocked. I don't want to digress but he told me that he needed some of my past tax returns to see if he could save me taxes when I realized that they were in my duffel bag which I left at Hampton Court in the garage. I then drove back to Hampton Court. I pulled up and picked up the intercom to call for permission to enter and no one answered. I tried to call three times and still no one responded. I took the remote out of the glove compartment of my car and it opened the gate. I pulled up to my old apartment and did not want to enter the house. I tried the remote for the garage door and it still worked. In the back corner on the right side of the building was my duffel bag. I was shocked seeing right next to it was the 1954 Cadillac Eldorado convertible which one of your employees said was at your house."

Bill Spaulding responded, "I left the car there since I didn't have enough space for it in my garage on Fitzwater Street and the new owners were fine with me leaving it there until I had room. Whoever told you that just assumed it was at my house."

Robert was relieved hearing that and understood that it certainly made sense.

"Do you know that I may wind up with absolutely nothing after paying the inheritance tax to both the State of Pennsylvania which they already took at settlement and what I might owe IRS?"

"Honestly Robert, I never had any thoughts about the ramifications of the transaction affecting you tax-wise. It never came into my mind."

"Forgive me for jumping to conclusions," Robert apologized.

"No problem," Bill said.

Robert felt mentally relieved knowing that his friend, agent and attorney had been forthright all along. After that Robert placed a call to his accountant leaving a message on his answering machine informing him that he had his previous few years of tax returns which showed minimal income and asked when can they meet?

While waiting to get a meeting together with his accountant he placed a call to Amanda Dillington. She also was not in her apartment and he didn't want to bother her at work.

"Call me when you get a chance. Looking forward to getting together." Robert left the message on her answering machine and 30 seconds later Amanda called him.

"That's pretty quick," Robert said as soon as he heard Amanda's voice.

"What's pretty quick?" she asked. Robert told her that he just left a message on her answering machine and she just called back. Amanda explained to Robert that she is still at work and didn't get any message. She told him that she was calling to see if he was in the mood for dinner when she actually wanted to confront him for never mentioning that he was the sole beneficiary.

"Wow! That's really coincidental because that's why I left a message asking you about getting together. Sure. Where would you like to go and what time?"

"How about Arthur's steakhouse let's say seven-thirty to eight o'clock ?"

Robert replied, "I'll be waiting for you at the bar at 7:30."

***

'You Should Never Change a Classic' read the sign displayed on the brick façade outside of Arthur's steakhouse at 1512 Walnut Street. Inside, the aroma of pan-seared steaks permeated the room. The rich dark walnut-stained wood panels enhanced the atmosphere. At the bar with its raised wood panels and a brass toe rail, the smell of cigar smoking overtook the smell of the steaks.

"I'll have a kamikaze and in a few minutes probably a glass of a rich oaky-tasting Chardonnay for a friend that I'm meeting for dinner," Robert informed the bartender. He was halfway through sipping his drink while he waited for Amanda and at 7:45 she tapped him on his shoulder.

"Hi. I hope I didn't keep you waiting. I'll have one of those also," she instructed the bartender.

"I was wrong. I thought you were going to order the Chardonnay from the Russian River Valley that you enjoyed so much and so did I." Robert reached for her hand to hold momentarily. It wasn't long before they both were ordering a second round. Before they could even start, the maître d' approached Robert to inform him that their table for two was ready and he'll send their drinks over to their table.

***

Amanda had serious conflicting feelings about Robert. She certainly enjoyed his company when she made dinner for him the comfort of him by lying by her side through the night. On the other hand, knowing what Detective Harrison told her that Robert did not divulge upset her significantly. She wanted to clear the air and was waiting for the proper time to approach the subject. The second drink made it easier.

"And what would your pleasure be tonight? The prime ribs? A sirloin strip?" The waiter asked.

"Everything is wonderful here," she informed Robert.

His eyes scanned the menu choices and he thought that his newfound wealth could afford this meal; however, this may be the last one that he could afford after paying his taxes.

The waiter confirmed the orders. "That's one New York sirloin strip Pittsburgh rare and one fillet mignon medium-rare. Mashed potatoes and creamed spinach and house salads for both of you."

"Robert, I have to ask why didn't you tell me that you were the sole beneficiary of Mrs. JP Moore's estate?" Amanda bluntly asked, since the second kamikaze made it easier for her.

He sat there with his mouth open both shocked and relieved since he wanted to get it off his chest and never knew when the right time might be. He told her exactly that.

"I felt so embarrassed seeing how successful you have been and what a failure I have been by chasing my dreams of being a famous actor. I've had butterflies in my stomach since that night we spent together. I had no idea that I was the sole beneficiary until after she was murdered. I did not lie to you when I told you that I cared so much for her. She treated me better than a good mother would treat her son. I worried about her every day knowing that she had a tumor in her brain but hoped that she would live forever. After I was with her about six months, there was a slight remission. She and her doctor both were amazed never thinking it would happen, but it did. I worked with her doing physical therapy and taking her out to dinner and kept seeing her improve—just a little bit—but she had been improving. The physical therapy that I gave her four days a week helped her significantly. She started walking better and didn't need her walker, only occasionally using her cane. I called up Detective Harrison at Upper Kellington Township, who is handling the case, and told him then I was in fact the sole beneficiary."

Before Robert could continue Amanda broke in. "Robert. You told Detective Harrison that you were the sole beneficiary?"

"Yes. I don't remember exactly what day it was but first I asked him if anything was happening yet with their investigation, which I had asked him several times prior. All he would say was that it is ongoing and he could not comment and then I told him," Robert emphatically stated.

Amanda was totally taken aback. Detective Harrison never told her that the only reason he knew that Robert was the sole beneficiary was strictly because Robert voluntarily had told him. It had nothing to do with the detective's investigative prowess. Harrison made it appear that it was information that he dug up and that Robert held back. She was very much relieved even though upset with Harrison. She believed Robert and was glad that she told him what was on her mind.

Enjoying their meals and cocktails they both felt better having had the discussion. Amanda started seeing her feelings towards Robert grow but as an experienced assistant district attorney she wanted to first verify with the Detective and confront him. She was ready to ask Robert to stay over at her penthouse again but another part of her mind told her to hold off.

Then out of the clear blue she asked Robert, "What's your agent and lawyer's name?"

To which Robert replied, "William Spaulding."

"Calhoun, Spaulding and Fiengold's Bill Spaulding?" she asked since she knew the firm as being one of the more prominent ones in the metropolitan Philadelphia area.

"That's him. The one and only I assume," Robert confirmed.

Chapter 13

"Detective Harrison, please. This is Amanda Dillington from the Philadelphia district attorney's office," she requested of the telephone operator.

"Harrison here, can I help you?"

"Yes, Detective Harrison. This is Amanda Dillington. We spoke last week in reference to the homicide of Mrs. JP Moore and you informed me that you discovered that Robert Snyder turned out to be the sole beneficiary of Mrs. Moore's estate indicating to me that he was your prime suspect. Am I correct?"

"You are correct," he responded feeling a twinge in his stomach that there was something else.

"Well I spoke with Robert Snyder just yesterday and he told me that he voluntarily told you that he was the sole beneficiary of the estate, yet you certainly implied to me that it was your investigative work that turned this up." She was blunt.

"I was pissed off. And I apologize for giving you that impression. I should've told you that it was in fact Snyder that informed me and not anything that either I or Detective

Simpson discovered during our investigation," Harrison sheepishly answered. "But the good news for your friend is that we are working on a lead that looks like it may be productive."

"I'm glad that you cleared that up because I was very upset thinking that you were misleading me. I wasn't trying to meddle into your case. I certainly have more than enough on my plate to take care of. May I ask what your new lead is?" Amanda queried.

"The physical therapist. We did a background check on her and discovered that she had been arrested twice and subsequently released with no charges. That stems from her association and live-in boyfriend, Tony Galloni, a known drug dealer. She's supposed to be in my office this afternoon since I have many questions for her. If you want, I'll be in touch with you or you can contact me periodically. Again, I'm sorry it was just a bad day for me and I felt that you were interfering but now I realize that you were just checking out things for a friend." Harrison was sincere in his apology.

"Thank you, Detective Harrison. My number is 215-676-7676. Just ask for Dillington. They will find me immediately. Again, detective, thank you for the update."

Amanda was relieved that Detective Harrison and his associate Detective Simpson had a person of interest other than Robert Snyder. It's not that he ruled out any possibility that Robert Snyder did it, but why would Robert ever tell the detective that he was the sole beneficiary if he was trying to hide anything? She made a decision to call Harrison at least once a week to see what progress if any he was making and was there anything that she could possibly do as an assistant district attorney in Philadelphia to help.

With everything going through her mind almost every third thought was about Robert and her personal feelings for him that have gone back many, many years. She used to enjoy being around him on a daily basis at Temple University whether they attended the same class or just passed each other for a brief embrace between classes. She certainly enjoyed their sexual relations and knew that Robert also did.

Had it not been for several circumstances that happened shortly after she graduated, would they have been a couple all through the years?

It made no difference, for shortly after they parted ways the year after graduation she met Clarkson and was infatuated with him. She never was certain that she absolutely and totally loved him since on occasions, even when they were first married, she thought passionately about Robert. She remembered a loving uncle of hers had once told her "Make the most of what you have and then you will realize that's pretty good." That stuck in her mind and although the years with Clarkson were pretty good, she felt that still was something missing. Was she missing her former relationship with Robert from years prior? These random thoughts ran in and out of her mind.

She was concerned that Robert would be upset that the prosecutor in her checking out everything he told her but she let it pass. It went with the job. "I should have had Robert stay over last night," she said to herself. Amanda decided to call him; however, there was no answer. She left a message for Robert on his answering machine, inviting him to share another bottle of Burgess Chardonnay with her. Then she regretted leaving that message when she should have just said "Hi. It's Amanda. Give me a buzz."

***

Back at Upper Kellington Township police department, while Detective Harrison was writing down a series of questions for the physical therapist, he was interrupted by Detective Simpson.

"Hey, Theo. Something just happened that might be a break. A squad car was following a Ford sedan on Monk Road that had a license plate which was falling off. He did a trace while following the car and discovered that the license plate was reported stolen. He approached the car with his flashers on and the driver slowed down and pulled over. Both the driver and the passenger were in their early 30s and Caucasian. There was no resistance. The officer asked for identification and registration for the vehicle. The passenger started to open the glove compartment; however, the officer already being aware that the tag was stolen, went back to his car and called for assistance. He instructed both the driver and passenger to not move and not get out of the car."

"Well?" asked Harrison and Simpson continued. "This is where it gets interesting. The second squad car came up quickly since he was patrolling in the area less than a mile away. At that point, the driver was instructed to get out of the car and put his hands on the roof. The second officer stood next to the passenger's door and told the passenger to slowly pull the keys out of the ignition and hand them to him. The passenger complied."

At this point Detective Harrison was starting to get upset. "Will you tell the story already?"

Detective Simpson gathered his breath. "The first officer asked the passenger to open up the trunk. He did. They found plenty of antiques but one stuck out in his mind. It was a golf tournament trophy presented to Mr. Rodney Moore, Mrs. J.P. Moore's deceased husband."

"Simpson. You just made up for screwing everything up." That was Harrison's way of congratulating someone. "Where are they now?"

"In the holding tank," responded detective Simpson with a smile on his face. "There is also a warrant for the driver's arrest in Philadelphia for a burglary. He's being processed now while the car is being dusted for fingerprints, especially everything in the trunk."

"Finally, we are making some headway. At least I'll have something to tell that Dillington in the DA's office."

Later Detective Harrison instructed Simpson to bring the suspect into the interrogation room. Once the suspect was seated, Harrison let him sit there for five minutes while a tape recorder hidden in the room was operating. After the five minutes, Harrison entered with a notepad and a pen. "I see you've been read your rights. I am going to be recording everything that we are discussing both my questions and your answers do you understand that?" Harrison asked.

"Yeah. I understand. I just don't know why I'm here. I didn't do nothing. You got me here simply because somebody gave me their car to use." Acting sarcastic Billy Thompson responded.

Detective Harrison then proceeded. "How old are you Billy?"

"Thirty-one."

"How did you come across all the antiques in your trunk when you were stopped by a patrol car?"

"That ain't my car. I got no idea who put that stuff in the trunk. It wasn't me," Billy responded.

"Well, you were stopped while driving an automobile with a stolen tag and inside the trunk were lots of antiques. Now, how did you get that car?"

"I told you and I told the two other cops it ain't my car I don't know a thing about it."

"Let's just quit the bullshit, Billy. Your fingerprints are on the items in the trunk. You've been arrested before and you know the routine. There is an open warrant for your arrest for burglary in Philly. The only possible way that you'll be leaving here will be after ten years to life in prison or just lay it out on the table and be truthful, but if you're bullshitting me you are in for a lifetime of problems." He continued, "Now tell me when you stole those antiques?"

"We were just riding in that neighborhood and I seen this house with no lights on so I figured I'll see what I can get. Maybe in this rich neighborhood there's something that I could hock. Albie, the guy with me, didn't want any part doing it so I left him in the car and I walked around the house and didn't see nobody in it so I looked around looking to find a window or door unlocked and found a side window opened about one inch. I opened it up and I was in some kind a dining room. I took the dining room table cover and I just wrapped up everything I could and got out the back door. I don't know how you guys got me so quick."

Detective Harrison fired back. "You say you got into the house through an opened window? You say you left through the back door why not the window that you came in? I told you Billy, no bullshit."

"I am not yanking your chain. I tried the windows and found one that wasn't locked. It was open about an inch. I didn't break into anything. I had this big dining room tablecloth filled with everything silver that I could find and could not get out the window since there was something holding the window halfway. I just about squeezed through it to get in. I went to the back and got out that door."

Detective Harrison picked up his yellow notepad and pen telling Billy Thompson that he'll be right back. Harrison was totally perplexed. Back in his office, he had Simpson come in and asked him to check if there any break-ins in that area recently. He thought that this petty burglar might just be a petty burglar but how is it that he had a trophy from the murder scene from months before?

Detective Simpson checked with the post board and there was no record of any break-ins in that area since the homicide of Mrs. Moore. That made things even more confusing. He knew that the trophy was obviously from the Hampton Court estate of Mrs. Moore. And he was getting upset since his gut feeling that Billy Thompson was confessing to a break-in was turning out to be wrong. With that, he walked back into the interrogation room.

"Billy, I told you, bullshit me and you're going to be serving plenty of time and it looks like that's how it's going to be. Tell me now what happened when you entered the Hampton Court estate and shot Mrs. Moore?"

"Oh no. No way, man. Don't give me that stuff. I don't carry a gun and I don't shoot nobody," he adamantly answered.

"If that's how it's going to be, you got a long stay," Harrison said as he was leaving the room but then stopped and turned around. "Why did you have that stuff in your trunk so long without pawning it?"

"Hey, Detective. You crazy? It wasn't 15 minutes later you cops pulled me over. How could I hock it so quick? I ain't no magician."

"Put him away and let him stew. Tomorrow call up Philadelphia and tell him we got him and see if they have any issues with his buddy Albie," Harrison directed Simpson, then added. "Are you sure this Albie comes up clean?"

"Nothing on him at all Theo."

"Simpson put a call into Robert Snyder. I want the inventory that was removed from Billy Thompson's car spread out, identified, and photographed. We need Snyder up here to identify these antiques. This guy Thompson could be trying to do a head job on us maybe because he realizes that he's a suspect in the Moore murder and by stating that he just stole these items that would throw us off the trail. When we were at the crime scene we saw no forcible entry but did anyone look to see if a window or door happened to be unlocked? Could've been left open on purpose? If so, who in the household would've left the window open? Maybe not someone that had the key but we have to check to see if anyone did work in the around the house who was not in Mrs. Moore's employ. Simpson, if he broke into someone's house why didn't they call the police to report it? Get Snyder in here as soon as possible."

Chapter 14

Amanda placed a call and got through to Robert on the first ring. "Do you have time to meet me at my apartment? I'm leaving work now. I would like to relax and have a glass of wine. Will you join me at three?"

"No problem. I was waiting to hear back from my accountant about how much, if anything, I will have after paying my taxes on the income from the estate and wouldn't mind never hearing from him. I'll head over to your place shortly."

This time it wasn't a surprise for Robert having a porter take his car and park it for him and the doorman acknowledging Robert's presence by tipping his hat while opening the door to the apartment building.

Robert knocked one time on Amanda's penthouse door and before he could think about knocking twice Amanda opened up the door with a glass of Chardonnay in one hand while she wrapped her other hand around Robert's back. She pulled tightly and kissed him. A surprised but welcomed Robert wanted more. He paid no attention to what she was wearing, simply enjoying her tight hug and kisses.

Then Amanda started rattling off with such exuberance he was taken aback. "I've been working six days a week for the past three months a highly classified case involving corrupt politicians within our city and quite frankly I'm exhausted. Shanahan, the district attorney, instructed me to take off for two weeks. I was thinking of getting back to my youth when I used to ride show horses and the one time that you and I rented a pair of horses and we went to the New York mountains for a week. Do you remember that? "

"Mohonk Mountain House around New Paltz, correct?" answered Robert.

"My mind has been so spinning that I could not think of that name no matter what and I didn't want to look it up in the AAA guide for New York State. Did you enjoy that week that we spent together? It was invigorating for me and we had some great sex."

"Of course I did," Robert answered. He was excited seeing that this was the same Amanda from his youth and he rattled off, filling her in on his past.

"I realize that other than my position working with Mrs. Moore, I stressed myself so much because I could not find a good-paying job in the theater," he continued laughing. "I could hardly find a bad paying job, so coming to work for Mrs. Moore was really a relief to me. I felt productive and my life had meaning to me. I was happy there and got acclimated to my obligations and responsibilities within just days. It really was comfortable and felt so good knowing that I was making her remaining time as enjoyable as possible. Seeing her improve thrilled me to no end and then her being murdered for some things they stole out of the house is beyond me. How anybody could do something like that has put my nerves on edge. Every day I feel a void not taking care of her. One should never take someone else's life."

"Robert do you want to go on a Dutch date and go back in time to Mohonk Mountain House with me?" Amanda brazenly continued. "I have a friend who runs the stable at

Mohonk and I know he will lend us two safe horses. What do you think?"

Robert was pleasantly surprised. At first, he wasn't sure if Amanda really cared for him and if the murder of Mrs. Moore made her suspect him. If she didn't believe that he was innocent of ever harming Mrs. Moore, she would never remotely suggest going to Mohonk.

He looked Amanda close up and smiled. "That would be wonderful. Just tell me what day you want to leave. I have no schedule to check for myself, so just let me know and I'll call up to make reservations."

"What are we waiting for? Every day means one day closer that I have to be back to work. Call information and get their phone number and let's see if they have a vacancy for tonight. If they do let's go. It's about 165 miles from here and probably take us three hours," Amanda issued her prescription for a relaxing week on the gorgeous grounds of Mohonk Mountain House with its sprawling Victorian buildings situated on the top of a mountain and surrounded by 40,000 untouched acres of paradise.

Minutes later Robert confirmed one room with a king-size bed for two for one week which was a honeymoon special rate even though it wasn't their honeymoon.

"I can run over to my apartment and pack my bag quick enough and head back here to pick you up," Robert told Mandy.

"Or you can look in Rodney's closet," she suggested. "Pick out what you want, as he was a conservative dresser and probably darn close to your size. He wouldn't mind and we can save some time."

"Honestly Mandy, I would feel uncomfortable. I don't want you looking at me and possibly seeing your husband. My apartment is only minutes from here on Fairmount Avenue and can be back here within 30 minutes with my own clothes. Bear with me," he requested.

"My car or yours?" she asked. Robert shrugged his shoulders and instead of saying it makes no difference he used one of his expressions from days at Temple, "*Mach schnell.*"

"Bring your car up to the front and I will inform the porter. He'll put it in my parking space until we come back. We'll take my car since it's already filled with gas. I'll meet you downstairs in a half hour. Go!" were Amanda's instructions to start a week of fun and relaxation.

Robert looked at his watch and confirmed he'd see her in 30 minutes downstairs. Amanda called downstairs as he left her apartment telling the Porter to bring up Robert's car immediately. When Robert exited the lobby the doorman told Robert to wait a moment while his car was on its way and sure enough it was pulling under the portico. He thanked the porter and headed to Fairmount Avenue, only a little over a mile away. He rushed up to the second floor and opened up his suitcase stuffing in a sport jacket one suit two pair of slacks one sport shirt one tie and one white dress shirt. On top of that four pairs of socks including one white set of underwear for the week, one pair of black shoes, one pair of loafers, and one pair of sneakers. "That's it." He said aloud to himself. As he started to leave the phone rang. He wondered who it could be. If it takes long, he would keep Amanda waiting and that's no way to start a relationship. That's what answering machines are for. Robert was in his car within five minutes and on his way back to Amanda's.

The phone kept ringing as Robert exited. On the eighth ring, the machine recorded a message.

"Mr. Snyder, this is Detective Simpson. We have two suspected burglars that we caught with antiques and that we would like you to identify as soon as possible. Can you get here now? If not, first thing in the morning? It's very important. Please call me or Detective Harrison."

***

As Robert pulled up his black Buick sedan, on the opposite side of the portico was Amanda's Mercedes waiting for him with the trunk lid open. This time as Robert got out of his automobile he immediately handed the keys to the Porter and reached into the backseat removing his suitcase.

Amanda came out holding a cup of coffee. "Just throw your suitcase in the trunk and let's go."

Amanda drove and Robert was quite comfortable sitting on the firm and perfectly stitched pleaded tan leather seats that appeared to have thousands of pinholes in the leather for better circulation. Sitting in the cupholder on the console between the seats was a fresh cup of coffee waiting for Robert. In the console was her car phone which was turned off. She slowly maneuvered the Mercedes through Center City traffic jams and got on the ramp for Interstate 95 heading north.

"Sit back and relax. This should be an easy drive from here. You read the AAA guidebook directions, but I think it's pretty cut and dry that we take this until we get onto 287 in Jersey. Then you'll have to tell me."

As they neared Edison, New Jersey, signs were posted for the Garden State Parkway. Robert instructed Amanda to take the exit as shown in the AAA Guidebook.

"Hmm, I thought that it was a straight drive right to route 287. I guess it just seemed that way," she said. She then realized that the last time she left from the Bucks County area and took the Tappan Zee Bridge in New York crossing the Hudson to Route 287.

She fought her way through the traffic leading to New York City area; it was a pain that she wasn't expecting. Living in Center City she was used to traffic congestion but New York's was trying her nerves. Exiting the Garden State Parkway, she took the road leading to the New York Thruway and then traffic flowed smoothly with the exception of a breakdown here and there. Even so, there was still daylight left as they entered the college town of New Paltz and drove up a long and winding road, which they remembered led to their destination: Mohonk Mountain House.

As Amanda pulled up in front of the main building, Robert was startled.

"This looks like an old age home. Look at them." Robert pointed to the Victorian porch where over a dozen very senior people on rocking chairs were rocking back and forth, the wooden chair's runners squeaking in harmony.

"I don't remember this being a retirement home," Robert alarmingly stated.

"Robert, cool out. We're here to enjoy ourselves and relax. Don't even pay attention. I think that it's charming."

A reluctant Robert opened the trunk and removed both their suitcases and a small bag belonging to Amanda. When he entered the building his attitude changed. Once passing the porch with the old people, he entered the reception area, a room of magnificent dark oak walls, oak carved columns surrounding staircases, and dozens of people seated in groups of two and four enjoying 'Teatime,' a tradition for more than a century at Mohonk. At least half of them were his age; many dressed in tennis outfits or jogging clothes.

"Now it all comes back to me. I remember this room perfectly. It was as gorgeous then as it is today," Robert mentioned as they walked up to the reception area and signed in.

Their room was on the second floor overlooking a majestic 17-acre lake, as if they were in the Swiss Alps. It was paradise just being here. Nothing to rush about here. Just take your time and enjoy your surroundings. The shower and bathtub seemed perfect for the building, not at all updated to anything modern but that was the charm of the place. The king-sized bed's mattress was extremely comfortable and soft as an overstuffed pillow. There was a champagne bottle waiting for them on the bureau that had been chilled in a silver container that was filled with crushed ice. A small try of handmade cookies lay on a silver plate, smelling so good that Robert and Amanda could not resist nibbling on them. A moment later the bellboy brought their luggage and pulled out a folding stand from the closet for one of the suitcases. Robert handed the bellboy a tip but before the young man left he asked, "Can I get anything for you, Mr. Snyder? Or for you, Mrs. Snyder? Perhaps logs for the fireplace?"

"Thank you. Yes." Robert closed the door after the bellboy exited.

"Assumptions in this day and age?" Amanda laughed. "I bet half the people here are not married."

Robert uncorked the champagne bottle, not paying attention to the vineyard or the vintage and with a *'pop'* the cork flew across the room, making Robert and Amanda both laugh.

Robert poured two flutes of champagne and picked up two cookies as he and Amanda sat on the plush Victorian sofa looking out the wraparound windows seeing mountain tops in every direction.

Just as they were getting comfortable bellboy knocked at the door, delivering strips of cedar for kindling the fire and graduated sizes of wood. "Can I start it for you?" the bellboy asked and simultaneously Robert and Amanda said, " Yes, and thank you."

The bellboy exited and Robert and Amanda, with drinks in hand, sat back again on the sofa watching the fire get stronger as they embraced.

"Mandy. I just cannot believe the relief of being out of the mayhem that I have been going through and the incredible pleasure of being here with you at my side. I think the last time that I felt this way was a lifetime ago, being with you back at Temple. Thank you for the great idea of us coming here and for you being you," Robert emotionally said.

"I've had an excellent life and all along felt that it was 90% of what I had hoped and dreamed of, saying to myself how much more could I expect? Yet all along I felt that there was still something missing that I would never experience." Mandy had tears in her eyes. "I'm experiencing it now. I think I love you."

"I hope that's not the champagne talking because if that's the case I don't know what you'll say when you find the little surprise hidden in my bag," teased Mandy.

"You don't! Do you? No. But, Ms. Assistant District Attorney, I hope you do."

93

Gene Epstein

With one hand around her waist and the other around her neck, Robert drew her to his lips and gave her a long, lasting kiss. His right hand slid down looking for the waistband of her skirt to slide his hand underneath and grab her.

"I do. Open up my pocketbook and find it if you can," she challenged Robert.

Besides a make-up kit, a tampon holder, a comb and a hairbrush, he found a 2 x 3-inch white plastic container holding eight joints of perfectly rolled marijuana.

"If you're ready, I am," she said.

He took one of the long match sticks, that were used to light the kindling in the fireplace, from its rectangular brass case and struck it against the hearthstone floor of the firebox. The elongated matchstick ignited immediately as he handed one joint to Amanda.

"Please, Mandy. Take the first hit."

Chapter 15

After stopping at the local sandwich shop for his early morning cup coffee and a poppy seed bagel sliced in half with mayonnaise on each side, detective Theodore Harrison wiped his face, left his usual ten percent tip, then headed to the Upper Kellington Township Police Department where his office was located on the lower level. Passing two patrol officers who were leaving since their shift was over, Harrison nodded without saying a thing and entered his office cubicle. The first thing on his mind was Simpson and his success in showing the stolen articles to Robert Snyder. his morning coffee seemed to have charged him up more than usual.

Instead of using the intercom, Harrison stood up and yelled over the partitions.

"Simpson! I need you now."

Shaking his head, Detective Simpson hurried into Harrison's office. "I called Snyder's number and only got his answering machine. I left messages three times letting him know it is important and to call me even if it's Monday. So far he didn't call, Theo."

95

"It's still early but we're sitting on these two and I'd like to still have control of them before Philadelphia sends someone here to get Billy Thompson. We might have to charge them both with burglary. Let's see what happens this afternoon and hopefully Snyder gets back to us. So far neither of them asked for an attorney and from the cash that they had in their pockets it doesn't look like either will have enough for bail," stated Harrison.

"Besides we already have their consent to tape-record what is an absolute confession to a burglary, we just don't know where it is and I don't want to drive them around to point out the house that they robbed. Any public defender, no matter how inept they may be, would tear us apart. Let's see how the day plays out."

As lunchtime approached there still was no return phone call from Robert Snyder which was concerning to Detective Harrison; however, Simpson did have some new information regarding Victor, the groundskeeper.

"It seems as though doing a background check everything came up clear under his name. I did background checks on all the other names that he went by and one popped up showing that he was arrested in Chester for a brawl and was held for four days paying a fine but no jail time," Simpson reported

"Big deal! That's it?" a sarcastic Harrison commented.

"No, Theo. It seems as though the fight with one Rico Rodriguez was over an argument about money that he was owed for doing something for Victor and when I checked out Rodriguez it turned out that he had been arrested numerous times for burglary and served a four year sentence and was released one month prior to Mrs. Moore's homicide."

"Well, Victor had a set of keys to the estate which we know and he never denied. Could he have worked with this other guy that he fought with to rob the place and it went wrong?" Harrison questioned. " Call over to Chester and find out if they have a location for this Rodriguez guy and let's see what we can get from him, if anything."

"And Simpson, put a call into Robert Snyder again and tell him it's urgent that he call immediately. If you don't get an answer back within an hour put a call into that assistant DA, Dillington, in Philly maybe she knows where he is. She initially called me since she is a friend of Snyder's."

"I have one of the detectives in Chester County checking for the whereabouts of Rodriguez on the phone," Simpson informed Harrison.

***

Two hours passed and Simpson had his hands filled working on two other cases and forgot to call Robert Snyder. As he was walking to the men's room, needing some relief from all the coffee that he had consumed that morning he realized it and turned around to place one more call to Snyder. He was frustrated because he was not getting any response from all his previous messages however he still left one more being very emphatic

"Mr. Snyder. I need you to call me immediately. Whatever you are doing stop it and call me now." Simpson then rushed to the men's room.

Another hour went by with no response from Snyder . Simpson then placed a phone call to the DA's office in Philadelphia to speak with assistant district attorney, Amanda Dillington. The operator told Simpson simply that "she's not available."

Simpson explained to the operator that he is a detective working on a case that she had expressed an interest in and would she be able to find someone in the district attorney's office to speak with that might help locate her.

"Let me find another assistant district attorney that may be able to help you, Detective Simpson," she graciously replied.

Simpson then spoke with another assistant district attorney and informed him that Amanda Dillington knew one of the persons of interest in a homicide. All he wanted to know is if he knew where she may be, since he needed to speak with her. He explained to the assistant DA that they needed that person to identify articles that they have in hand at the

97

Upper Kellington police department, which may have been stolen during a homicide.

He was informed that Amanda was on a two-week vacation. Her car phone number was not available; however, her penthouse phone number was given to Detective Simpson.

Simpson immediately placed a phone call to Amanda's apartment and once again an answering machine picked up. He left a detailed message and requested that she respond as soon as possible noting that they are holding two suspects and goods stolen from what appears to be Mrs. Moore's estate.

After that, he focused his attention on two other cases that he's been actively involved with and minutes later the operator at the Philly DAs office called Simpson to give him Dillington's personal car phone number since they realized the urgency.

"Thank you so much, and please thank the assistant DA for me for providing her personal number."

He then placed a call to her car phone. It rang and rang and eventually went to what he thought was an answering machine but he simply got disconnected.

Being frustrated was nothing unusual for a detective. Actually, it was quite the norm. Simpson then had a temporary reprieve when a detective in Chester County called him with the whereabouts of Rico Rodriguez. Rodriguez was now supposedly living in Trenton, New Jersey, and Simpson was provided the address but no phone number. Now Simpson would have to figure out when he could break away to drive to Trenton, which was a good hour away, without knowing if Rodriguez would even be there.

Chapter 16

Amanda acquiesced and gladly took the first hit of the joint. She confessed to Robert that this packet of a rolled joints was in her freezer for well over a year. A friend of hers had encouraged her to take a couple hits when she needed to relax after a tough day at the office; however, she never did.

It just sat there next to low sugar ice cream and a package of frozen peas, waiting for the proper time

"I hope this didn't lose its potency," she told Robert as she inhaled for the second time and handed the joint to him for his pleasure.

"Just being here with you Mandy, away from everything else, is a hell of a high to start with. Whatever potency remains is just a plus."

In his right hand he held the joint that Mandy had just passed to him and in his left hand was the flute of chilled champagne. He inhaled once and coughed a few times almost choking and laughing at the same time, then to soothe his throat he took another sip of the chilled champagne. Robert inhaled deeply and held it for a count of ten and exhaled looking at Mandy and smiling, like some silly teenager overwhelmed being on his first date.

They both became very quiet. Robert removed his shoes, then lay back and placed his feet on the cocktail table in front of the overstuffed Victorian sofa, which was like a cocoon surrounding both of them. It seemed like an eternity before either one of them spoke a word although it was only one minute or so. The kindling wood worked its wonders and ignited the split oak logs giving off a gorgeous view of all imaginable colors flashing in front of them; as the fire grew in its intensity, the flames of love and passion grew proportionately between them.

"I can't remember if I ever felt the way that I feel now. Being here with you cuddled up in my arms I will treasure the rest of my life. Mandy...Mandy, I think I'm in love. Not infatuation, but real love."

"It must be the pot," she smiled hoping that he would disagree. "Bobby, it is you. You are what I have missed out on in my life ."

While both of them were still holding a flute of champagne in one hand they managed to embrace on the sofa. Robert drank the last ounce while holding Mandy tightly to him and put his glass down still embracing her. Reaching forward he offered to take Mandy's and place it next to his.

With the champagne bottle and two empty flutes sitting on the cocktail table, Robert slid off the sofa onto the floor, encouraging her to do the same. Mandy gladly got on the floor next to Robert while she pointed to the fireplace.

"Great idea Mandy, let's lie next to the fireplace," Robert agreed.

With both of them laying on the floor together, each with one arm around the other's back watching the mesmerizing dance of the flames from the oak logs, Robert was surprised when Mandy rolled him onto his back and unbuttoned his shirt. Her kisses went down his neck and back around each of his ears sending vibrations through his body. He then rolled Mandy onto her back and unbuttoned her blouse following suit. His kisses from the nape of her neck to her breasts and circled around each areola sending Mandy's body into tremors. All of a sudden there was a knock on the door. They looked at each other somewhat petrified and buttoned up quickly. Robert got up and shouted in a loud voice, "I'll be right there," wondering who it could be.

Robert removed the safety chain then slowly opened the door to find a man in his 70s wearing a burgundy velvet smoking jacket with black lapels holding smoking a pipe.

"I'm so sorry to bother you; I'm on the wrong floor," he apologized and left.

Both Robert and Mandy looked at each other then started to laugh. Robert did not realize that he never placed the 'do not disturb' sign on the outside of their room. Neither of them knew what to say to each other. Was the mood lost?

"How about if we take a shower and head downstairs?" Mandy questioned. "I think they serve dinner late."

"Might as well," Robert responded. "You first?"

"Not at all. Let's do it together." Mandy smiled.

The bathroom was is a typical Victorian layout with a large white porcelain tub and many chrome-plated plumbing fixtures on the wall, making the tub useful as a full shower. It had a draped silky white sliding curtain hung above from a semi-circle chrome plated rail to prevent water from the shower splashing onto the black and white one and a half inch alternating octagonal floor tiles. Opposite the tub was a white porcelain toilet that had a chrome plated pipe running up the wall to a container several feet above which held the water for flushing. The toilet seat was dark oak stained wood.

Instead of turning on the shower, Mandy let the tub fill up. "Just wait," she said as the tub reached halfway Mandy lifted one leg carefully holding onto the side of the tub while she brought her other leg in and sat down.

"How about washing my back, Bobby?"

Without hesitation, Robert looked down at her gorgeous body and her breasts halfway submerged and reached for the soap and sponge to wash her back. She looked up at him and was glad to see that he had an erection. Moments later, he carefully got into the tub facing Mandy.

They were both in a world of their own. She was away from the mayhem that she faced minute by minute working in the district attorney's office, being there to answer questions and ask questions constantly. He was removed from the trauma of the woman that he cared about and took care of having been murdered, leaving him with no direction for life.

Robert carefully sponged every part of Amanda's body, making certain to emphasize her erogenous zones. As the sensations built up in her body she took the sponge from Robert and started to wash his body, in particular his erection. Chills ran up and down his spine. He could not remember ever having such feelings of desire nor being with someone that he totally loved. As she was going to engulf Robert's erection he pulled her away and kissed her instead. A kiss that seemed to go on forever... after that, he turned the shower on and they both rinsed each other off with the flexible corded shower hose.

While both had passionate sexual desires, they realized that the dining room would be closing within a half hour and they both were starved.

"I could go on all night but I think we should both grab something to eat. I can smell aromas of sizzling steaks. Does that work for you?" Robert cautiously asked.

"Bobby, we have just started. A good meal it's hard to turn down. Just keep that erection for when we come back," she coyly responded.

Robert reached up for the chrome heated towel rack and removed two very large bath towels wrapping one around Amanda and the other around himself. They dried each other thoroughly even rubbing each other's genitals more than was necessary. Moments later they were dressed and heading downstairs for dinner.

"A table for two," Robert instructed the maître d'. He seated them at a window overlooking the wondrous lake below while handing both of them dinner menus and the wine list.

While Amanda's eyes were perusing the menu, Robert was looking at the food plates on surrounding tables wondering what looked the best to eat. He did not however ask anyone if they enjoyed what they were eating, even though he was tempted to do so. He did not want to embarrass Amanda. Then he asked her what she was in the mood to eat.

"I was tempted when we were in the room but I don't see your erection on the menu," she joked.

"I'm all in for the New York sirloin strip, Pittsburgh rare. And you?" Robert said.

"I think I'll have the pan-seared trout almandine stuffed with scallops and shrimp."

The attentive waiter came moments later and confirmed that they made wonderful choices and suggested a 1974 Hanzell Pinot Noir paired with his sirloin strip and a Chablis for her trout. Robert looked at Amanda with a shrug.

"The Pinot Noir sounds excellent and that should still go well with my trout," Amanda said. The waiter did not argue.

Hors d'oeuvres were sent to them, compliments of an unknown admirer, which seemed strange because no one knew they were even coming nor did they even know until hours before. That certainly did not stop them from consuming them while enjoying the Pinot Noir. They were like kids on their first date enamored being in a company of someone special.

After thoroughly enjoying the house special soup of wild mushroom bisque sprinkled with crushed cashews, their entrées were served. Robert's steak came out on a skillet still sizzling and done to perfection. Amanda's trout also came out on a hot skillet and was placed on her plate exactly as described, surrounded by hand-whipped mashed potatoes and freshly picked buttered baby peas. After finishing their entrées, both being filled to capacity, they turned down the gorgeous dessert tray, opting for plain black coffee. Robert surprisingly suggested taking their coffees with them to the outside porch.

"Robert, you shock me. You wanted to leave when you saw people sitting in those rocking chairs on the porch and that's where you would like to go and have our coffee."

"It looks relaxing. Sometimes things aren't what they just appear to be," he said as they brought their coffees out to the porch.

The early spring evening chill was apparent and both of them felt it. Moments after they sat in the rockers, a maid brought them warmed blankets so they could enjoy the outside while being comfortable. Moments later, Robert stopped rocking as his eyes closed and he dozed off. Mandy was so relaxed she didn't realize that almost that two hours had passed when the maid brought both of them replacement heated blankets.

"Thank you, but no. It's not necessary. We're going to head back to our rooms." Amanda reached over to give Robert a gentle tug when he said, " I'm up. I must have just closed my eyes for a moment."

They both returned to their bedroom and fell asleep.

***

The following morning at 6:30 a.m. Amanda was in the bathroom brushing her teeth while Robert remained sleeping. The sounds of water running from the sink and one of the water pipes that had air in the line causing it to rattle awakened Robert. He looked to his right and Amanda was not in bed when he realized the sounds that he heard were not coming from an adjacent room but the bathroom. He walked in while she was brushing her hair and coming up behind her, gently lifted his Tee shirt that she was wearing and embraced her with both his hands meeting on her moist pelvic triangle, instantly giving him an erection. She felt it pushing against her buttocks and reached around with one hand grabbing it, sending Robert's nervous system to new heights.

Letting go, she never turned around when Robert gently pulled down her black and white checked panties exposing her buttocks but leaving them on. It turned him on looking at her gorgeous backside and he took some harmless baby bites on both cheeks, not to hurt her but to send chills down her spine. It worked for both of them. They returned to the bed and after nearly one hour of foreplay and sex with

104

multiple orgasms Amanda suggested they go for breakfast downstairs .

"We both just had plenty to eat of non-caloric value over this last hour. I think it's time to consume some calories. The smell of bacon is making me hungry." Amanda conveyed her sense of humor.

They washed up quickly and dressed in jeans, planning to go horseback riding after a walk to the top of the mountain.

Downstairs in the main dining room, the air was filled with the scent of bacon enough to make anyone hungry.

They were seated at the same table as the previous evening and a young waiter presented them with menus, followed by a busboy bringing them carafes of regular and decaffeinated hot coffee.

"Does the Chef have anything special that he recommends for breakfast?" asked Amanda

"Our chef recommends his favorite omelet of Norway kippers with onions, diced green peppers, and scrambled eggs."

Robert asked, "Can't he make the eggs very runny and not folded like an omelet?"

"Of course. The chef is very accommodating. And you Mrs. Snyder?"

She didn't correct the waiter or tell him that she is Mrs. Amanda Dillington, thinking that people will believe that she's cheating and did not want to go into any explanation.

"I'll start off with oatmeal and maple syrup then an order of the Canadian bacon with sunny side up eggs. Oh, I almost forgot, your fresh orange juice first and toasted whole wheat bread with my eggs."

"You will both enjoy your breakfast here this morning, I assure you. Anything that you may think of, please let me know and it will be taken care of for you." The waiter removed both menus from the table as he backed up bowing his head and headed to the kitchen with their orders.

"I'm glad I didn't take my beeper so that we are not bothered even though I do feel a tad guilty not calling into the office or to my apartment to retrieve messages."

***

Thirty minutes later they were both satisfied in every sense of the word from their morning experiences both in the bedroom and in the dining room. Feeling totally refreshed they decided to go to the stable, which was a quick walk away, to check out the horses. Amanda in her youth was an avid hunter and jumper enthusiast taking lessons weekly at a horse farm in Huntington Valley. At one point she even started driving horses that pulled antique horse-drawn carriages. Robert had only experienced an occasional trail ride on a rental hack horse from a stable on Dumont Avenue in the Roxborough section with trails that meandered through the woods of Wissahickon Park.

Tony, the stable manager, was impressed with Amanda's equestrian background since most visitors knew nothing about horses. He told her that on occasion, the Carriage Association of America and the American Driving Society held events here that brought people from as far west as California to the north of Canada for annual weekends. He explained how horse trailers pulled up with magnificent well-groomed and highly trained driving horses that pulled antique horse-drawn vehicles and had competitive events on the property. Providing that she signed a waiver of liability, he had at her disposal, an antique carriage that could be pulled by either one or two horses.

"Robert, would you want to try this? I know you never have before, but I can handle either a single or a pair if that's okay with Tony."

"Sure. Let's do it if you're comfortable. I'm only going to be a passenger."

Tony nodded. "I have a good pair for you that know every trail, so you'll never get lost."

"Do you have a good single horse?" asked Amanda

"I certainly do. He is an American Saddlebred named Stonewall Commander. Let me show him to you. " Tony cordially replied.

Then Tony brought out from one of their larger box stalls a handsome horse with a coat that shined like a copper penny with a flaxen colored mane and tail. He had an almost perfect white blaze that ran down the center of his head and into his nose. All four of his feet had white socks that rose about ten inches above his hooves making him a gorgeous specimen.

"I just call him Commander. He's the best of the best."

"Do you need any help getting him hitched up?" Amanda asked.

"Not at all, ma'am. If you come back in 20 minutes, Commander will be groomed and hitched for you both."

Amanda was very excited to be driving a horse once again and was confident in her ability. She suggested to Robert that they go back to the dining room and order a box picnic lunch for their trail drive with Commander.

When they returned to the restaurant Robert was very surprised to see that they actually had a menu for Boxed Picnic Lunches. He chose the egg salad sandwich with chopped olives on a hard Italian roll. Amanda chose the deli combination sandwich. In addition, they each ordered one apple and a bottled beverage. The package was placed in a gingham cardboard holder. Robert then looking at Amanda, ordered a split bottle of Zinfandel, which included a complimentary Mohonk Mountain House corkscrew and two wine glasses to be returned. At the same time, a man in his 50s was returning a small English wicker picnic tea set from the Victorian period and thanking the dining room employee for the use of it.

"Would you care to use this for this afternoon?" The employee asked of Amanda.

"Take your pick of the various tea selections and crumpets." He opened up a mahogany box filled with numerous choices of imported English teas.

"Thank you so much." She picked out a couple of packets of Earl Grey tea.

They then went to the stable.

"Your carriage awaits," Tony graciously stated. "This is Commander. He understands everything that you ask of him."

Tony stood in front of the horse holding him by the bridle as Amanda stepped up and into the carriage. She held the reins with her left hand then instructed Robert to place his right foot on the step plate and his left foot on the floor of the carriage and sit down to her left. She was given the map of the entire mountain trails leading to Skytop, which was the pinnacle of the mountain.

"Here we go. Nice and easy Commander. I have not driven horses for ten years or more, so let's go easy." She spoke to the horse as he walked slowly leaving the barn and heading towards the first trail.

At first, Robert was not sure how capable Amanda might be after many years since she last drove a horse and carriage but within a quarter of a mile, he was sure of her competency. The gingham lunchbox and the English tea set were placed behind the front seat on the floor of the carriage. Also, there was a plaid picnic blanket rolled up secured by two leather straps behind the seat.

The narrow dirt trail meandered up the mountainside. As they got higher they were at eye level with the tops of the pine trees. That caused Robert to get icicles in his knees because he had a fear of heights even though he was on the inside and not looking to the right and down 75 or 100 feet as was Amanda. She was capable and having a wonderful conversation with Commander. By 11:30 that morning they reached a plateau and Amanda drove into the open field.

They got out of the carriage and Amanda with Commander's reins in her hands, walked up patted him on his neck, and rubbed between his ears. She placed his halter on and removed him from the harness and carriage. Holding the horse by the lead line attached to his halter, she and Robert took a walk through the grass field looking at mountains in the distance. She found a large chestnut tree and Robert decided to remove the blanket from the carriage and spread it on the ground while she attended the horse. The weather was beautiful. The sun was out with very few clouds and just a light breeze which was perfect for the spring jackets that they wore. Robert brought over the picnic box and tea set, which he opened. Removing a striker match he lit the alcohol heater and placed the already filled sterling silver teapot in the bracket over the flame. He then took out the packets of Earl Grey tea and placed them into a delicate China cups while waiting for the water to boil.

They were certainly in no rush. How beautiful it was they agreed, looking over the world from such a quiet and tranquil place. From where they stood they could see that the trail circled the mountain going to Skytop. There was a seating area where one could see the gorgeous lake beneath them, forming its half-moon shape around the base of the mountain.

Amanda took out one of the apples and cut it in half with utensils supplied in the lunchbox. She sat on the blanket with Robert while she still held on to the lead line. She then asked Commander if he wanted to taste the apple and he bent his head down to eat it out of her hand.

The three of them were alone picnicking under the chestnut tree. No one could be seen in any direction. As the water came to a boil Roberts thoughts were of Amanda and making love to her right there. Amanda, without realizing what was on Robert's mind, secured the lead line to the chestnut tree. She sat down to pour the tea for both of them when Robert looked at her closely and she saw what was coming. He took the teapot from her hand before she poured out the hot water and returned it to its base. Leaning towards her, he pulled her to him and laid back with her on the ground.

"What's on your mind? As if I don't know," asked Amanda.

Moments later, with her blouse unbuttoned and her jeans down, his kisses sought every part of her body. It was reminiscent of the '50s movie *Picnic* with William Holden and Kim Novak. As the water boiled, over so did their sexual arousal all while Commander stood watch.

When Commander started to whinny they both looked around and saw several people on horseback coming off the trail and heading towards them. Thankful for such a smart horse, they buttoned up as quickly as possible and reached for the sandwiches as if nothing was happening.

At this point having company in close proximity, the mood was lost, so they finished eating their picnic lunch and organized everything, placing their 'lookout' Commander back in his harness and into the carriage after rewarding him with the remaining one and a half apples.

They were back on the trail and heading to Skytop. As they came close to reaching the summit one couple driving a horse in a two-wheel natural wood cart approached from the opposite direction. Both Amanda and Robert looked a bit uptight as the opposing carriage approached. The other driver looked absolutely petrified. Something had to give.

Amanda had her wits about her and told the driver, "Pull as far right as you can so that I can pass you." Which she did, with no problem.

A very short time later they reached Skytop and stopped the carriage but did not get out.

"I think I've had enough sightseeing today how about you, Robert?"

"Let's get back down and head to the bar. I could use a drink."

Less than one hour later, returning Commander to the stable and thanking him for a safe drive up and down the mountain Amanda handed the reins to Tony who had a fresh straw bed awaiting the horse's arrival.

Sitting at the bar both toasting on freshly made kamikazes they heard thunder in the distance. Amanda asked the bartender if there was a storm on way and he confirmed that the next three days the weather called for several inches of rain in the area with occasional bolts of lightning.

"Well, it's been great here the past couple of days and we have thoroughly enjoyed being here and I particularly look forward to driving Commander once again," Amanda said to the bartender.

Robert agreed. "This is a difficult place to leave."

After two additional drinks each over the following hour, both of them were just thinking of closing their eyes and grabbing some sleep. When they got to the bedroom Amanda looked at Robert and said, "Please don't get upset but I want to check my answering machine at home." She did without any objections from Robert.

There were six messages left for her, including three from Detective Simpson requesting the whereabouts of Robert because they need him urgently to identify items that they believed to have been stolen from Mrs. Moore.

Amanda informed Robert and even though he was ready to hit the sack at 4:30 that afternoon he placed a call to Simpson.

Ironically Simpson was not to be found in the building. However, hearing his name paged detective Harrison picked up the phone.

"This is Detective Harrison, Detective Simpson is unavailable at this time. Can I help you?"

"Yes, Detective. This is Robert Snyder. I just received word that Detective Simpson may have items for me to identify that may have been stolen from Mrs. Moore's estate.

"That is correct Mr. Snyder. How soon can you get here? We are holding two suspects on burglary charges and want to confirm the items which were stolen. Can you get here now?" he requested.

"Detective Harrison, right now I am in upstate New York and will be returning tomorrow morning. Is that OK with you?"

"I'm so glad to hear from you, Mr. Snyder. Please be here as early as you can tomorrow morning. Either Detective Simpson or myself will be here."

Taking Interstate 87 South at 9 a.m. the following morning, traffic was moving smoothly even though the rain was coming down quite heavily until they traveled about fifty miles when traffic came to a halt. The road was being cleared of a four-car collision while gawkers on the northbound lane slowed down to watch. Fifteen minutes later they were back on their way but a bit slower due to the weather.

Amanda placed a call to her office to tell the DA that she cut her vacation time short but was feeling refreshed and would be in early in the afternoon. Robert used the car phone to call his answering machine at his apartment only to hear urgent calls from Detective Simpson and one from Boyle, Boyle, and Bernstein the accounting firm.

She drove to her Center City apartment building and instructed the attendant to bring Robert's car to him. Amanda realizing that Robert was in a hurry to get to the Upper Kellington police department to see the stolen article, reached over and kissed him.

"I really do love you, Bobby. I hope that they really have Mrs. Moore's killer. Please let me know what is happening. " She then had her suitcase brought up to her Penthouse and changed clothes before heading to work.

Chapter 17

"I'm here to see Detective Harrison," Robert told the young woman at the counter opposite the front entrance of the police department. "Please tell him that Robert Snyder is here."

A moment later, coming from a stairway to his far right, the door opened and a grateful Detective Harrison reached out in total sincerity to shake Robert's hand.

"Glad that you are here Mr. Snyder. We have been waiting anxiously for you for several days. Can you follow me?".

Harrison opened the stairway door and walked down one flight of stairs to his section motioning to Robert to follow him. They walked down a hall passing numerous office cubicles to a small unattended evidence room. Harrison signed in and time-stamped a card with his name on it.

On a long table covered in white paper to contrast with the items recovered in the stolen automobile driven by Billy Thompson, were about a dozen items. In the center was the golf trophy presented to Mr. Rodney Moore. Most of the items both left and right of the trophy were sterling silver antiques.

Robert stood there looking but had no positive recollection. "I'm sorry Detective but I really can't be sure. They may have been there, but I am not certain. Mrs. Moore

113

had China cabinets that I assume were full of valuable items, but I never paid any attention to them since I had no interest."

"But Mr. Snyder, you had to notice this golf trophy. Did you read it?" a frustrated detective asked Snyder.

"I see it was presented to Mr. Rodney Moore but perhaps it was in another room on a shelf? It obviously came from Hampton Court."

"Will you testify under oath that it came from Hampton Court, the home of the deceased Mrs. Jacqueline more.?"

"Gladly, Detective," Robert confirmed.

Detective Harrison brought Robert up to date with recent developments. "A police car pulled over two people driving an automobile with a license plate that was hanging loose. While following the automobile the officer received confirmation that the license plate had been stolen. The officer called for assistance and subsequently pulled over the two suspects driving the car which also turned out to be stolen several months prior. The license plate was just recently reported stolen from another vehicle. The officer requested that one suspect open up the trunk of the automobile at which time the articles that we showed you were in the trunk. They both were arrested and fingerprinted.

"The fingerprints of one of the suspects driving the vehicle matched all the articles. The interview was tape-recorded with the consent of the suspect, who subsequently admitted that he entered the house through an unlocked window on the first floor on Monk Road finding no one home and removed these articles. The second suspect we believe did not participate in the burglary however he remained in the automobile at all times according to both of them. When questioned about a 22-caliber pistol both suspects adamantly denied owning a gun.

"When we looked at all the articles we saw the golf trophy that was awarded to Mr. Rodney Moore and that rang a bell. In addition, there was no reported burglaries in that area. We believe that Billy Thompson, the driver, disposed of the 22-caliber pistol. We needed you or someone else familiar with these items to identify them as being from Mrs.

114

Jacqueline Moore's home to charge them initially with burglary (18 Pa. Con. Stat. § 3502.) which Billy Thompson already admitted to.

"There will be a preliminary arraignment tomorrow at 10 a.m. It will be held at the Magisterial District Court in Narberth on 707 Montgomery Avenue where the charges will be formally entered.

"I request that you be present to at least identify the trophy as coming from the home of Mrs. Jacqueline Moore should they assign him a Public Defender. Otherwise, it is just a formality reading of the charges and the defendant's response. It will be quick.

"I know they will not be able to post bail so they will probably be held at the Montgomery County jail until the next hearing. At least that will give us more time to tie them to the murder."

***

Robert called Amanda but had to leave a message. "Hi, Amanda. I miss you. I really do. I met with Detective Harrison but only one of the items that they found in the thief's car rings a bell. He asked me to be at the arraignment tomorrow in case he wants me to speak with a public defender that may be representing the two thieves. Other than that, it's supposed to be quick and a formality but I'm sure you're well aware of that. If I didn't drop out of law school I would've known more about the process. Can't wait to see you. Love you."

The following morning Robert Snyder met Detective Harrison as he was entering the Magisterial District Court at 9:45.

"No one will be calling on you to testify since this is just a preliminary arraignment, but I wanted you here in the event there is a public defender representing Billy Thompson and Albert Young. I wanted him to see that you are here and have identified one object that was definitely stolen from Mrs. Moore's estate."

115

Moments later, after two quick procedures, the case was completed. The bailiff called out, "The Commonwealth of Pennsylvania versus William Thompson and Albert Young."

At that point, the district attorney informed the magistrate that Albert Young and William Thompson are being charged with burglary statue 3502. And that William Billy Thompson has an outstanding warrant for burglary from the City of Philadelphia. The magistrate looked at both defendants and asked them if they understood the charges. They nodded in confirmation and then he asked if they have an attorney. He also informed them that there will be no bail for William Thompson since there is an outstanding warrant for him and $25,000 bail for Albert Young.

"If you do not have an attorney or cannot afford one, we will have a public defender meet with you," instructed the magistrate.

Detective Harrison, after a brief conversation with the district attorney, Harold Mazor, told Robert that there will be another hearing for probable cause when the State has to show the judge that they have enough evidence to go to trial.

Harrison also told Robert that at least these two thieves will be in jail while they build a murder case against one or both of them.

Robert assured the detective that he would call him once a day, shook his hand, and left for his car. Once he opened the door to his Buick sedan, he reached the center console and lifted the car phone handset out of the receiver to return the call from Garrett Paul Boyle Jr., the accountant. Garrett asked him to come to his office immediately. Robert told him that he was just leaving the arraignment hearing for two suspects in Mrs. Moore's death and that he would be there in less than 30 minutes since it would not be much out of the way to his home.

Robert exited the District Court on Montgomery Avenue and headed South to Bryn Mawr Avenue trying to avoid traffic and hopped onto 76 S. taking him into Center City to the office of his accountant. After he parked his car, he entered the office building and pressed the elevator for the second floor then looked office Suite 201.

As he entered a secretary sitting behind a half-round counter asked him "Are you Robert Snyder?" Robert simply confirmed. " G.P. is expecting you." She pointed to the office to her right.

"Garrett, I'm here. What's the bad news?" Robert extended his right hand to shake G.P.'s.

"Robert, sit down. I'll lay it out plain and simple. If the property that you inherited had not been sold within six months you would have been responsible for an inheritance tax for the fair market value of the property and its contents, plus the valuable antique automobiles. From my calculations and contacts with real estate appraisers, they place the value in the $2 million range on the estate, not counting its contents. There was a caveat that stated currently the market for such estates is minimal and the only buyers are investors willing to wait and take the chance that the market turns around. So on one hand it was good that you did sell the property and did so quickly prior to holding it six months."

Robert looked quizzical. " Well, tell me, after reviewing my previous tax returns, what is the bottom line.?"

"Being that you inherited a property and are non-related to the deceased you are in a tax bracket at 39% of the proceeds. It is up this year to 41%, however, you did close this past December. There is $124,000 exemption from whatever proceeds that have been received. The sale of the property including the contents is recorded as $750,000. The value of the automobiles is $150,000. If we just use those figures there would be 39%, which is $302,640. due to the IRS. The settlement sheet shows that you paid debts, which reduced your proceeds, however, your personal debts are not a tax deduction therefore doing it properly you owe the IRS $302,640. as of today."

Absolutely astonished, Robert felt like he was going to pass out. "At settlement, I received $332,000 out of everything and you're telling me I owe almost all of that and it has to be paid immediately or else I have to pay a penalty?"

"Correct. However, since the automobile titles were never transferred into your name and you simply handed them over to pay a debt I think that we should just record the sale of the estate for $750,000. I must inform you that there is a slight chance that the IRS might pick this up during an audit and then you would be responsible to pay," GP continued. " Leaving out the automobiles saves you $58,500. It's up to you. As far as I'm concerned, if it was me, off the record I would do it that way."

Robert then asked, "How much do I have to write the check for?"

"$244,140. today. I hope you have it."

Robert sat there disheartened, pulled out his checkbook, and wrote out a check to the IRS for $244,140.

"Robert, since we are not reporting the non-registered automobiles I will file an amended Pennsylvania Tax return requesting a refund due you in the amount of $22,500. I will contact the title company first to see if it has yet been filed."

Robert could not believe ever having that amount and now seeing it disappear so quickly. After spending money for an apartment and some minor personal items, Robert was looking at approximately $80,000 remaining and hopefully another $22,500. He took a deep breath after signing the check and the IRS forms then reached over and shook the hand of Garrett Boyle Jr.

"I have some decisions to make and I have a good idea what they're going to be." Downtrodden, Robert then left the office.

Leaving the offices of Boyle, Boyle and Bernstein, Robert headed north on Broad Street until he reached West Montgomery Avenue. He then went straight to the School of Law at Temple University to reapply hoping that he would have credits for his first year. It had been many years since he left law school. He was told that he would have to start over; however, his previous four years in Liberal Arts, which afforded him a bachelor's degree, still counted. He was asked to fill out forms and return as soon as possible. Thirty minutes later, never leaving the building, Robert returned with his forms completed and presented the paperwork to the secretary at the school of law. He was then informed that they will process it and get back to him with a confirmation. The secretary of admissions saw absolutely no problem and gave him the date when classes would commence.

Robert left elated and relieved. He could not wait to contact Mandy and tell her that his life finally had direction.

With the remainder of the funds, after paying all his bills including the payment to the IRS, Robert had enough money to fund the next three years of law school, pay his monthly rental payment, utilities, food, and auto insurance with a little left over. A part-time job would keep him afloat with no pressure.

Gene Epstein

Chapter 18

"Hi ,Amanda. I have some news that I'm anxious to share with you. If you're home, please pick up the phone." Robert waited a few seconds and hung up, then he placed a call to her office, hoping that he would not be bothering her but he was extremely anxious to share the news.

"This is Amanda Dillington. May I help you ?"

"Amanda. It's me. I can't wait to see you and bring you up-to-date. I feel like a new person and I want to share it with you," Robert, excited, spoke rapidly.

"Can you tell me what it is? I'm on the edge of my seat."

"What time are you coming home? I can meet you there." Robert paused. " I really want to tell you in person."

"I can be there at 4:45."

"Great. I'll be there."

With a couple of hours to kill Robert drove to his apartment and picked up the mail. He made a cup of coffee. There were a few advertisements forwarded to him from the Moore estate by the post office and a bill for the car telephone since it was put in his name, even though the estate was paying the bills. The telephone bill was a notice of shut off for nonpayment. He didn't care since the phone was primarily used as a comfort for Mrs. Moore when he drove her to her

120

various appointments and dinners. Then he thought to himself with the arrest of the two suspects in Mrs. Moore's murder perhaps he should have use of the phone in case the detectives need him and he's not at home. He was concerned about having another expense after he had figured out most everything to be covered.

"I'll keep it for another month or until this case is over," he said out loud even though no one else was there. In a way, assuring himself that he was doing the right thing and not being extravagant.

At 4:30 he drove his car to 1700 Rittenhouse and was greeted by the porter and the doorman who got to know him from his frequent visits to see Amanda. They must have realized that Robert was not there on business, since he and Amanda were always hand-in-hand, acting like lovebirds.

At 4:45 Robert knocked on the door and Amanda appeared holding two flutes of champagne, one in each hand.

"Please tell me what's going on. I've been on pins and needles waiting to hear."

First, he told her about the preliminary arraignment of two suspects in the murder of Mrs. Moore. That, so far it seems as though one of the two entered the house and stole articles. "The detective wants me to be in touch with him often in case I am needed. They only charged the two with burglary since they don't have enough evidence at this time to charge them with murder in the first degree.

"After the hearing, I left and went to the accountant to see if after paying the IRS inheritance tax, I would have anything left. He figured out that I would have about $75 to $80,000, plus I would be due a refund from the Pennsylvania State inheritance tax amounting to another $22,500. Then, I decided it's time for me to change my direction and I drove immediately to Temple University to re-apply to law school." Robert hesitated, gathering the courage to continue.

"If you are willing to wait until I graduate and get a position at a law firm, I'd like us to be engaged. I think about you 24 hours a day. Not just passion and love-making but being with you. I've never felt such a joy in my life; that's why

I decided that I want to be self-sufficient and go back to law school."

Amanda just looked at him. They both stood just a few feet away from the doorway; Amanda still held both flutes of champagne.

"Robert, I'm shocked. I know how we've been getting along so great and I do love you, but you're going to have to give me time to think about this."

Robert reached for the champagne, somewhat elated that she did not reject the idea but at the same time a bit disappointed that she would not commit.

"Let me look at my watch. Hmmm. I think that's enough time. Oh my God, Robert, yes. I am so happy. I love you so much. I think about you all the time. I can't wait to see you. And now with you going back to law school, you will feel so much better about yourself."

They put down their champagne glasses on a side table and hugged each other for what seemed to be an eternity. She had tears in her eyes and with one hand wiped them away.

Chapter 19

Two days after the preliminary arraignment detective Harrison received a phone call from Marcus C. Reilly Esq., the court-appointed public defender in the case of the State of Pennsylvania versus William Thompson and Albert Young Junior, informing him of his representation.

Detective Harrison being somewhat upset said, "Wait till we get them for murder."

Attorney Reilly expressed his concern and asked Harrison if they could have a meeting to discuss this.

"Anytime you want, counselor. You tell me."

The following day Marcus C. Riley, Esquire appeared at detective Harrison's office in Upper Kellington Township. He was young and used that to his advantage to appear naïve when he was probably more intelligent than the detective.

"This is one of my first cases Detective Harrison and I want to do my best to protect my client's interest. I realize there is an outstanding warrant in Philadelphia for him for a burglary but that's not any bearing on what we have here."

Detective Harrison felt totally in control and possibly let his guard down. "We already had a positive identification on one of the articles that was stolen from the estate of Mrs. Jacqueline Moore on Monk Road in Gladwyne. This is the same Mrs. Jacqueline Moore that was murdered during the commission of a burglary. Your client on his own volition agreed to be tape-recorded and admitted his entry into the property and the theft of antiques that were found in the trunk of his car."

"Wow! It looks like do you have a hell of a case against these two. If you don't mind can I listen to the confession?" the public defender asked.

"Gladly, counselor." Harrison stood up and shouted over the partitions between the cubicles "Simpson, bring me over that tape recording of Billy Thompson's confession."

"I'll bring it right over. This damn key keeps giving me problems with my desk drawer."

Less than a minute later Detective Simpson handed Harrison the tape recorder with the enclosed tape marked 'Thompson confession.'

Simpson left and Harrison started the recording for public defender Marcus Reilly. Reilly appeared shocked that his client actually admitted to gaining unlawful entry into a private residence and removing numerous antique items mostly all being silver. Reilly then asked who identified the objects that were purportedly stolen to which Detective Harrison told him that it was the person in charge of managing the estate for the past two years.

"You said, Detective, that one of the objects which was stolen was identified. How about all the others? Were they not identified?"

Harrison had no answer. Then he said, "The property manager of the estate certainly doesn't look into every closet and nook and cranny when he's overseeing the entire property."

"That's very understandable, detective but how is it that he identified one object? Can you show me what that object was?"

"Follow me to the evidence room."

In a small back room with a heavy-gauge metal wire latticed frame enclosing a counter no one was attending, the detective took a key off his keychain and unfastened the

Master lock. On the bench covered in white paper were all the objects that were found in the trunk of the stolen automobile driven by Billy Thompson and his accomplice Albert Young Jr.

"So Detective, out of all these objects your witness was only able to identify one? And which one may I ask?"

Detective Harrison pointed to the golf trophy that was engraved as being presented to Rodney Moore.

"It looks like you've got him, Detective. Do you think we can work out something with the DA for my clients?"

"Counselor, we are looking to prove that either one or both of your clients committed murder during a burglary," Harrison felt cocky talking down to the young public defender. "They both should face life imprisonment or the death penalty."

Reilly then asked if either of their fingerprints were found on the premises since the report shows that the fingerprints are on the objects in the trunk of the vehicle it seems obvious that neither one of them wore gloves.

Harrison looked straight at the young attorney without a word. A moment later, he said they must've entered the premises but removed them after they left.

"Detective. Did you find any gloves for either one or both of them?"

"Negative," Harrison replied.

"I'm also a bit confused that you say that you're looking to find them guilty of the murder of Mrs. Moore which happened several months prior to them being apprehended by a local patrol car."

"That's right, counselor. The items stolen were from the premises of the murder."

"Detective Harrison, if a pawnshop sold this particular trophy to a customer would you claim that that customer, the recipient of a possibly stolen article, committed murder?"

He continued, "Did you ever check to see where either one of my clients were the day of Mrs. Moore's murder?"

Detective Harrison realized this young public defender was no dummy that he could manipulate; he had no answers for Riley's questions.

"Also detective, how was Mrs. Moore murdered?"

"She was shot with a 22-caliber bullet right in her head. Dead on the spot."

"Detective Harrison, did you find a 22-caliber pistol that belonged to either of my clients?"

"We have not, counselor."

"I hope to see you at the probable cause hearing next week, detective. It has been a pleasure. Thank you for your time. By the way, I would get Detective Simpson's evidence drawer repaired," he said sarcastically.

Harrison wondered if this young kid was playing with his mind.

***

As promised, later that day Detective Harrison received a phone call from Robert Snyder checking in. Harrison informed Robert that they'll be a probable cause hearing the end of next week and told Robert that he would like him there in the event that the district attorney needs him to make a statement regarding the trophy from Mrs. Moore's estate. Without any hesitation, Robert assured the detective that he would be there. Robert also gave the detective the car phone number telling the detective that he will keep it operational until whoever did kill Mrs. Moore is convicted.

***

When the public defender Reilly returned to his office he had the file pulled from Philadelphia to find out what, if any, legal representation Billy Thompson had regarding an open warrant for his arrest for burglary. Then he made arrangements to meet with his clients at the Montgomery County prison the next morning to go over everything that they said and was said to them.

The next day Reilly drove to the Montco Correctional Center on Airy St. in Norristown parking at the courthouse facility assigned to attorneys. He registered at the front desk and was given a temporary identification card. About ten minutes later both of his clients were brought into a secure room with a long desk and four chairs. A correctional officer stood there while Billy Thompson and Albert Young Jr. were seated. The public defender then looked at the officer and asked for privacy. The officer closed the door behind him remaining in position outside of the door.

"You both have a serious problem. The detectives have your tape-recorded confession," he told Billy Thompson.

"You were both apprehended driving a stolen automobile with a stolen license plate and stolen goods. You are both implicated in the murder of Mrs. J.P. Moore," Reilly continued. "Is there anything I'm missing?"

"You bet. That's a lot of bullshit. We didn't kill nobody. I don't even have a gun. I never owned a gun. I told that to the detective," Billy yelled.

"Tell me, Billy. When did you steal the automobile?"

"I didn't steal it. I wrecked my car and a week before Christmas I rented it from a guy in the bar for fifty bucks but he didn't have a registration so I kinda figured he stole it. Then after paying him for a month, he disappeared so I didn't have to pay anymore. The tag expired so I stole one."

"Now tell me, when did you break into the house and steal the trunk load of silver?"

"Is somebody crazy? I told the cops that fifteen minutes after I threw everything in the trunk, I was just driving down Monk Road and I see a cop behind me flashing his lights. I got no idea how they caught me so quick".

"You did not steal these items in December and keep them in your trunk until the police caught you?"

"No. That's crazy. Why would I keep that stuff in the trunk for all those months?

"Well, for one, the detectives believe that if you sold the items and they wound up in a pawnshop that would tie you to the murder."

"What happened in Philadelphia that there's a warrant for your arrest for burglary?" asked Marcus Reilly.

"I don't know. I didn't rob no place for a couple of years and that was a nothing job that wasn't even reported to the police because the guy was a crook that I grabbed some shit from. He'd be afraid to call the police."

"I'll check with Philadelphia to see if I can get an explanation of the warrant for your arrest. I need to know—and this is extremely important—was anyone in the house when you broke in?"

"If there was anybody, they were deaf. When I went to tie up the silver in the sheet a big coffer pot slid out and landed on the floor. I almost shit myself figuring if anybody was there they would've called the police immediately and I didn't want to see anybody. I just wanted to get my ass out of there as soon as possible." claimed Billy.

"Now, Albert, the police said that you were the lookout while Billy broke in. Is that correct?"

"Nope. I knew what Billy was going to do and I told him he's crazy I don't want anything to do with it. I just went out with him for a joyride." Albie responded. "I didn't stop him. He made up his mind. He told me he was broke and needed a couple hundred bucks."

"One of the items has been positively identified as coming from the house on Monk Road where the murder took place. How do you explain that?" Reilly asked.

"I can't." Billy shrugged his shoulders. "I got no idea."

"Next week there will be another hearing to show probable cause. I believe that the district attorney on the information supplied by the two patrolmen and the two detectives will have no problem bringing this case to trial. They might ask at that time for the charge to also include murder in the first degree."

A stunned Billy sat there almost in tears. "Honestly. You gotta believe me. I didn't kill anybody. No one at all."

Chapter 20

"Simpson, what were you able to find out about any of our suspects previously owning a 22-caliber pistol?" asked Detective Harrison.

"No good, Theo. I ran everybody's name through the National Crime Information Center and their records just started. Prior to 1980, everything was only entered by hand and even though dealers were required to keep records of any sales for 20 years, we would have to go through every dealer's records. With all the countless registered dealers it could take years. Finding that information is nearly impossible since we would have to know who the selling dealer was and then check record after record by hand to see if they ever sold to one of our suspects. Without the actual serial number on the pistol we are at a dead end."

Detective Harrison had an idea. "How about you ask anyone who had access to the house at Hampton Court what they did with a 22-caliber pistol that they owned? Implying that we know that they owned one. If they deny it, then state we really want the truth because we know that they did have one."

"But Theo, what good would that do?"

"What do we have to lose? Maybe one of them gives us some bullshit story or just denies ever owning one," Harrison responded.

***

Over the next three days, Detective Simpson contacted everyone that had access to the Hampton Court main house. He did not want to do any questioning over the phone and made arrangements to meet each of them starting with Stasha, the housekeeper. They met at her apartment off of Edgemont Avenue in Chester Pennsylvania at 6:30 that evening. It was an exhausting experience trying to get her to understand what he meant when he questioned her.

"What did you do with the 22-caliber pistol that you owned?"

She just looked at him as if he were talking gibberish. He then asked if anyone there spoke English and she brought out a friend or an acquaintance named Adam. He wasn't much of an improvement but he did understand detective Simpson's question. In Polish, he asked her.

Stasha shook her head saying, "No, no, no."

Moments later, Detective Simpson left their apartment.

The following day in the early afternoon he met with Joanne Lawrence, Mrs. Moore's physical therapist. She was between visits and welcomed him. She claimed that she never owned any type of handgun but when she was young her father gave her a 12-gauge shotgun and she had no idea where it is. Leaving her he went to meet with the attorney for Mrs. Moore's estate, William Spaulding Esquire, at his office in Center City.

The conversation was totally turned around when Bill Spaulding inquired as to how their investigation was going and was there anything that he could do to aid them?

Without discussing the case, Detective Simpson simply asked Bill Spaulding what he did with the 22-caliber pistol that he owned.

"I have over a dozen handguns but do not own a 22-caliber," Bill Spaulding responded. They are so small and ineffective that I find they have no use. If you want a handgun for protection you should have a 38 caliber Smith & Wesson Chief's special."

Detective Simpson left and then contacted Robert Snyder and asked where he could meet with him.

"I'm in Center City," Robert responded, "is there a place that's convenient for you?"

"Pick a place" Simpson said. "I can be there in 30 minutes."

"How about if we meet at the new McDonald's on Broad Street near Girard Avenue?"

"I'll see you there in a half-hour."

Robert was there before Simpson. He ordered a coffee and sat down at a table. About fifteen minutes later, Detective Simpson arrived apologizing that there was an accident holding up traffic on his way there.

"That's not unusual. Living near Center City I see it every day. How about a coffee for you?"

Detective Simpson ordered a large black coffee and brought it back to the table.

"In doing background checks on everyone that had access or worked at Mrs. Moore's property, we found that you owned a 22-caliber pistol. Where is that pistol now?"

"Wow, Detective. You're certainly doing a thorough job. It has to be nearly ten years since I've even seen it. I kept it under my pillow when I was hanging out with two other unsuccessful actors sharing a small apartment. I didn't know either of them personally, I was just paying one third the rent for about six months until I moved out. Then one day I needed some cash and I sold it to a pawnshop for $25."

Robert continued, "What's happening with those two burglars? Did they have the gun that killed Mrs. Moore?"

Detective Simpson could only give his canned speech. "This is an ongoing investigation and we cannot reveal the details at this time."

Detective Simpson headed back to his office after leaving a message for Victor, the groundskeeper, at the last property where he was working, to contact him.

Simpson then sat down with Detective Harrison to discuss what they have to do next to move forward with murder charges.

"We have the body. We have the ballistics report and the bullet. We do not have the gun. We should discuss this with the DA since we don't want to hurt our murder case," Detective Harrison suggested. "I don't want to be embarrassed at this point in my life."

Harrison placed a call to the district attorney Harold Mazor going over everything that they had and telling the DA that his gut feeling is that these two committed murder during a burglary. He explained that they do not have the murder weapon but they do have positive identification of the personalized trophy that was awarded to the husband of the deceased and was found in the trunk of the stolen vehicle driven by the two defendants.

"Number one, we have a purported felon with an outstanding warrant for his arrest. Number two, he was driving a stolen automobile. Number three, the stolen automobile had a stolen license plate. Number four, and probably the most important, is one of the stolen goods that has been definitely identified as coming from the scene of the homicide, was found in the trunk of the vehicle driven by Thompson and accompanied by Young.

"As far as I'm concerned, Detective, you did a good job and I don't think that there would be a judge that will not let us proceed to trial. We certainly can show probable cause. Then the real kicker is William Thompson's tape recording where he admitted to committing the burglary even though he was smart enough not to mention anything about a homicide."

The district attorney continued, "The only thing that doesn't add up is the timeline. He admitted to a burglary that he claims happened 15 minutes before the police caught him. To date, there has been no one reporting a burglary of the items found in the possession of Thompson. Why was he driving around for several months after the homicide with incriminating evidence in his trunk? I need you, detective, to gather more information to support that the stolen objects were stolen the day of the murder of Mrs. Moore."

"Mr. Mazor. I really don't know what else, beyond what we have done, we can do."

"Get a search warrant for his Philadelphia address and check every single thing possible. Hopefully, you'll find the murder weapon. In the meantime, I will place a call to the court clerk to ask the judge to give us another week. They won't object."

"I'll do that immediately, Mr. Mazor. We will come up with something," Detective Harrison assured the DA.

"Simpson, get me somebody in the DAs office in Philly to see if they can get us a cooperative judge to issue a search warrant for Billy Thompson's residence. Tell them that we have William Thompson in custody and that when we're done with him we will gladly escort him to Philadelphia to appear for his outstanding warrant but it looks like he will be staying here in prison for a long time."

***

That Friday Detective Harrison made a compelling argument to a Philadelphia Court Judge the Honorable Seth Clayton stating that there is an open warrant for William Thompson for his arrest from the City of Philadelphia for burglary. The same William Thompson had also burglarized a home in Gladwyn and admitted it. William Thompson was apprehended driving a stolen Ford sedan with a stolen license plate affixed to it. One or more articles that were stolen from the property and discovered in the trunk of the stolen vehicle was later positively identified as coming from a home on Monk Road where several months prior one Mrs. Jacqueline Phyllis Moore was shot in the head with a 22-caliber pistol. Detective Harrison requested a search warrant limited to finding the murder weapon, a 22-caliber pistol, from William Thompson's last known address: a second-floor apartment on Dounton Street in the Germantown section of Philadelphia.

133

At 3:45 p.m. The Honorable Seth Clayton issued a search warrant for the second-floor apartment occupied by William Thompson limited to seizure of one 22-caliber pistol and any items known to have been stolen.

The timing was not conducive for a search of the apartment since 4 o'clock was the shift change for local police in Philadelphia. Detective Harrison, hoping to get back to the office in time to check out himself, requested two Philadelphia police officers meet him with a battering ram at the premises exactly at 10 AM that Monday.

Everything was arranged and Detective Harrison drove back to his office in Upper Kellington with the search warrant, first entering the evidence room using his access key. Moments later he exited and placed the search warrant in the top drawer of his desk, locking it. He then contacted DA Mazor to inform him that Monday he will execute a search warrant along with two police officers. After that, he went home to relax for the weekend.

***

From the moment he left Upper Kellington Township Theo Harrison, as much as he tried, was unable to clear his head of all the thoughts about Billy Thompson being the killer of Mrs. Moore. He knew his instincts were correct almost every time, so he knew he didn't want this case to fall apart. As far as he was concerned, he had to look no further knowing that they had the murderer in their custody. His concern was this young seemingly naïve public defender Reilly.

When Monday came he was ready to call the office telling them that he was heading straight to Philadelphia when he realized he had to go back to retrieve the search warrant in his desk. Even with heavy traffic, he was still there by 8:45. His secretary brought over two messages for him and after reading them he returned one call.

Shortly after finishing his cup of coffee, he left for his 10 o'clock appointment with the search warrant.

Expecting to find two patrolmen he saw two highway patrol cars outside on Dounton Street instead and approached one of them.

"I'm Detective Harrison; you guys have the battering ram?"

The two officers wearing bulletproof vests and protective headgear exited the car. The one holding the battering ram said, "Detective, please show me the search warrant before we enter."

Harrison obliged.

"Let's go!" he ordered.

Harrison followed the two officers to the front door and knocked. To his surprise, an elderly woman opened the door.

"Can I help you officers?" she graciously asked.

"Yes ma'am. We have a search warrant for Billy Thompson's apartment on the second floor," Harrison told her.

"You got to bust in his door?"

"Yes. Unless someone opens it," Harrison replied.

"Don't do that. You'll damage the door and I can't get any help to fix anything. How about if I give you the key? Where's Billy been? I haven't seen him for over a week. He's such a sweet young man."

Detective Harrison explained that Billy Thompson is being held in custody in Montgomery County and the search warrant was to his apartment on the second floor.

It turned out that the elderly woman has been living there for over 50 years and for the last decade has been renting out her second-floor apartment.

Harrison took the key she gave him and, with two of the officers, went to the second floor and knocked on the door first not knowing what to expect. No one answered. They waited about 15 seconds and knocked once more, stating they were the police with a search warrant for the apartment Billy Thompson. No one answered so Harrison simply used the key to open the door.

Once inside with one officer standing in the doorway, Harrison instructed the other officer to check out the bedroom and bathroom while he checked out the kitchen and living room. Systematically, each one took apart one drawer after the other looking in cabinets, closets, even tearing a bed apart and lifting up carpets. Harrison suggested that they switch places to be sure nothing was missed.

Harris looked through the bedroom again while the other officer checked out the living room and kitchen.

The police officer yelled, "I got it!" He held a 22-caliber pistol by a pencil in the trigger guard.

"Where did you find that and how did I miss it?" a puzzled Harrison asked almost embarrassed not having found it himself.

"It was behind the second drawer in the kitchen cabinet."

"That doesn't make sense. How did the drawer close all the way if the gun was behind it?"

The police officer then opened the drawer and showed Detective Harrison that the drain from the sink had a serpentine curve and that the drawers were made shorter by 3 inches in order to close properly. The apartment previously was just the second floor in the house with no kitchen and later fitted out as an apartment. The two lower drawers were modified during installation to accommodate a drainpipe.

Elated, Detective Harrison placed the gun in a plastic bag and thanked the woman and the two officers then drove back to his Upper Kellington office.

Once he returned, he looked like a kid that was just given the keys to a car for his 16th birthday. He entered smiling, held up the plastic bag, and announced, "Someone's going to the electric chair."

He looked around and asked if Captain Erickson was there or at some function.

"No, he's out with some of the commissioners again," said someone behind a cubicle.

"Will someone check this in?" said, still holding the gun for everyone to see.

"Use your key, Theo. I'll witness the check-in," Simpson offered.

Excited, Harrison then placed a phone call to district attorney Harold Mazor informing him that the search warrant yielded the 22-caliber pistol that they were seeking.

"You should be proud of yourself, Detective. You did a thorough job. Adding a murder charge will be my pleasure. In the meantime, get in touch with ballistics so they can match it to the bullet extracted from the victim."

About 2:30 that afternoon Detective Harrison received his almost daily phone call from Robert Snyder as promised. This time he had great news to give Snyder.

"Mr. Snyder, we just found the murder weapon hidden in Billy Thompson's apartment."

"Wow! That's great, Detective." Robert felt relieved. "I can't wait to let everyone know. Can you tell me what's next?"

"Right now it's up to the DA. He'll contact the court to get a date for the hearing to show cause and there will be no one better prepared than him," Detective Harrison happily said.

Chapter 21

Totally relieved, Robert Snyder immediately called Amanda to tell her that the murder weapon was found in the apartment of the burglar. He left the message on her answering machine. He then called his friend, attorney, and former agent who was not at the office. Darlene, the agent's new secretary, told Robert that he left early today to relax and work on one of his favorite cars. Robert assumed that he was at his garage on Fitzwater St. but the secretary said he was at his home in Bala-Cynwyd.

"Even with all the help he has at his garage when Mr. Spaulding gets stressed out from his workload, the only way he seems to relax is by working on one of his antique cars by himself."

"Do you think he'll mind seeing me? I have some great news for him."

"Not you, Mr. Snyder. He always talks about you."
***

Leaving his apartment on Fairmount Avenue, Robert drove to the Schuylkill Expressway and stayed on it until he reached US 1 then turned left heading to Bill's English Tudor styled home nestled in the center of a 5-acre wooded lot off of Monument Avenue. Over the years Robert had been there several times and always admired the home that was built in the early 1900s. The immediate grounds surrounding his home were impeccable and the large woods gave Bill the privacy that he so much needed. A well-paved driveway meandered through the wooded lot into a Y. Taking it to the right brought you in front of the house and to the left, the drive led you to the garage behind it. A large swimming pool was to the rear of his house but positioned so that the trees would not interfere with the sun nor drop leaves in the pool. About 75 feet to the left of the pool was a stone two-car garage in the same English Tudor style. A flagstone walkway adorned with English boxwood on both sides connected the house to the swimming pool and the swimming pool to the garage.

Robert entered the driveway slowly and respected the cast-iron sign requesting '10 MILES PER HOUR.' He took the left lane which brought him to the garage where Bill's car was parked outside. Both garage doors were closed. Robert saw the lights were on and went to the door to the right. As a courtesy he knocked on the door.

"Who is it?" Bill asked.

"It's me, Robert. I have some great news."

"Come in but be careful I'm under here, working on the brakes."

"Bill, are you crazy? With all the help you have you're getting yourself greasy working under this Gullwing? You have a brand-new car lift downtown, but you are using these antique jack stands?"

"It's my only relaxation. And you know how much I've always loved this car. I want to get it ready for a car show. I don't have much time to work on this but I find some excuse to leave work. I get great satisfaction doing this myself. What's the good news?"

"They found the murderer and the gun that he used to kill Mrs. Moore. It seems as though there were two people. One was an accomplice while the other went through the house to steal silver and killed her."

"That is great news. Exceptionally great." Bill maneuvered himself from beneath the automobile lying on a wooden mechanic's roller creeper. He got up and went to embrace Robert but stopped before he ruined Robert's clothing with his greasy hands. On the wall behind Robert was a container of Go-Jo hand cleaner and on the table alongside was a pile of rags. Bill squirted the cleanser onto his palms and rubbed his hands, then wiped them using a clean rag. He hugged Robert.

"When did you find out?"

"Just today. About every other day I put a call into the detective that's been working on this case trying to get any updates since they found some objects that were stolen from Mrs. Moore's house. They have two people in jail now who admitted burglarizing the home and I identified a trophy that was awarded to Mr. Rodney Moore for his golfing prowess that they found in the suspects' possession. Today, when I called in, was the first time that the detective felt positive that they have the murderer and his accomplice in custody." Robert continued, "They got a search warrant for one of the guys that they have and they found the 22-caliber pistol that they were looking for."

"They killed a sweet and caring old woman who was helpless strictly to rob her house. I hope they get executed," Bill exclaimed.

"Me, too. It can't be quick enough."

"By the way, I have some more news," Robert rattled off. "I went to Temple University to see if I could get my credits from the first year of law school since I've decided to go back and get a law degree. They informed me that it's been so long that I'd have to start again but I really want to and I figured that I have just enough money to get by until I graduate and get a job. Maybe with a firm like yours?"

"You're full of good news today. I'm thrilled to hear that you're going back to get your law degree. And if you keep your grades up the way you did in the past I'm sure my partners and I would agree to give you a position here. Or I can recommend you to a judge for a clerkship. Either way, I'm very proud of you."

"If it wasn't for you, Bill, I would still be dreaming about becoming a famous actor but the reality is that I finally have come to my senses, albeit ten years late. I will be a good lawyer. No one's going to study harder than me."

Robert looked at his watch and wanted to tell the news to Amanda in person. He said his goodbyes to Bill and could not stop thanking him. Once he got into his Buick sedan, he picked up the handset to call Amanda in her car since she should be leaving from work and heading home. The phone rang several times with no answer. There was an accident on the Schuylkill Expressway, so Robert sat in traffic for about 30 minutes until the tow truck pulled off one of the vehicles. Once the traffic was cleared up he was on his way to 1700 Rittenhouse to see Amanda.

At 1700 Rittenhouse, the porter smiled and opened the door for Robert, at the same time giving a young couple directions to Independence Hall.

When Robert reached Amanda's penthouse he knocked twice and in a flash the door opened.

"I got your message but I didn't drive today. I decided to walk because the weather was lovely. What brings you here today? Not that I'm not thrilled to see you."

"No kiss? I'm the guy that's going to marry you. Unless you changed your mind?" Robert was half-joking.

"I'm so sorry. I picked up my answering machine and saw that you tried to reach me and I tried calling you on your car phone but the call never went through. Are you OK?"

"They have the killer," Robert said, visibly excited. "They got a search warrant for the burglar Billy Thompson's apartment and there they found a 22-caliber pistol. Something that he denied ever owning."

"Robert, I'm so glad for you. Now, if this isn't an inappropriate time it never will be." She and Robert kissed for an extended period of time.

"I just came from Bill Spaulding's house to give him the good news and he was happy as could be. You wouldn't believe it but he was working beneath an old Mercedes that had tiny jack stands holding the car, instead of taking to his shop to be worked on. He told me that's his therapy when he breaks away from work. Anyway, it feels great knowing that it's over."

Amanda opened up her wine cooler and brought out a bottle of Cabernet Sauvignon. Robert uncorked it and filled two glasses halfway. They sat on the sofa.

"I know how you feel, Bobby, but this can go on for a long time. I know you are excited but there are so many things that get processed and numerous times there's conflicting testimony it never seems that it's ever going to end. And then when you finally think it has ended somebody will file an appeal. Just be happy and play every day as it comes."

Chapter 22

Marcus Reilly was informed that the murder weapon was found during a search of William Thompson's second-floor apartment. The district attorney has added the most serious charge yet—murder in the first degree against both defendants. Upon being notified he headed directly from his office to meet with his clients Billy Thompson and Albert Young Jr. at Monto County prison. His first concern was meeting with Billy, who was brought into a secure office with a prison guard standing at the door. Reilly broke the news and was a little bit upset with his client. "You lied to me. Of all people you should not lie to me; I'm the only one that can help you. Why did you tell me that you never had a gun when they found it at your apartment hidden behind a drawer ?"

"That's total bullshit! I did not lie to you. I never in my life owned a gun. I don't like them. I feel safer without one," a panicked Billy answered.

Reilly asked, "Does anybody who lives with you own a gun?"

"No one. The last person that stayed at my place was over six months ago and he hung out for two weeks while he was going through some battle with his wife. And he wouldn't own a gun."

"You have a problem, Billy. It looks like they are holding all the cards. Now with the gun that they found there's a good chance that the DA asks for the death penalty."

"I swear to God. I've never owned a gun in my life. I don't know how they found something that I don't own."

Reilly pulled out a calendar and asked Billy where he was day by day from December 1 until the present. Billy was not much of a help. He admitted that he's not a good drinker and some days he just doesn't remember the day before. After a half-hour taking notes on Billy, he called in for Albie Young and sent Billy back to his cell.

There was absolutely nothing that he was able to extract from Albie other than he admitted that he was there with Billy when Billy stole the silver but wasn't with him when he got the Ford sedan that they were both driving. He kept swearing that the police pulled them over right after Billy robbed the place.

Something was gnawing at Reilly. Why would these two admitted thieves state the same story that they told the police that they were apprehended 15 minutes after they left the property on Monk Road?

Reilly went to all the hangouts that Billy mentioned to him and spoke with bartenders and waitresses, trying to get some insight on Billy. There wasn't one person that thought that Billy would ever kill anyone. They always saw him back down from a fight. And when he got drunk he was a nice drunk. The worst thing they ever mentioned about him was the couple times that he did get drunk and one of the guys in the bar insisted that they drive him home. Even one time after he fell and broke his wrist he still wanted to drive home.

Reilly contacted the DA and asked what for a plea deal and the DA laughed at him.

"Before we found his gun I would've made a deal. Now no deal. See you in court."

During the following two weeks and before the next hearing, Marcus Reilly checked and double-checked everything that he was told by both Billy Thompson and Albert Young Jr.

***

"All rise. The Honorable Seth Clayton presiding," shouted the bailiff.

In the courtroom were both defendants, detective Theo Harrison and Detective Simpson with public defender Reilly. The courtroom was filled with reporters from the Philadelphia Inquirer and all the local television stations. The rest of the seats were taken by visitors.

The district attorney read off the charges of murder in the first degree during the commission of a burglary against William Thompson. Each one was being tried separately, Billy Thompson first. The public defender Marcus Reilly announced his presence.

One by one, the prosecutor took the judge through each step that led to the additional charge of murder in the first degree. He also played a tape recording of Billy's confession over the objection of the public defender, who stated that this was done without the presence and advice of an attorney and under duress.

"Your Honor. I object to anything on the tape recorder since it was not kept in the evidence room following the chain of command but in the desk of a detective. Anything on that recorder cannot be used as evidence," stated Reilly.

"Overruled, counselor. It was in a secure position in the detective's desk."

The prosecutor then played the beginning of the tape when detective Harrison asked him if he realizes that this is being tape-recorded, which Thompson acknowledged. The judge told the prosecutor to continue even though the public defender was furious. They called Robert Snyder to the witness stand and he was sworn in. The prosecutor asked Snyder if he in fact could identify one or more of the items that were found in the trunk of the automobile driven by Billy Thompson. Robert Snyder confirmed that a golfing trophy that was presented to Mr. Rodney Moore was probably from Mrs. Moore's home. Upon closer examination, public defender Reilly asked Robert if he remembered where it was displayed. Robert said he could not remember. Then Reilly asked why he was unable to identify even one other item out of the nearly one dozen and he told the judge that he didn't remember seeing them in the house during his two-year stay there but they could have been.

"Could they have been somewhere else?" Reilly asked. "Someone else's house? After all, you were there two years and you can't remember seeing any of these items. Is that correct?"

The prosecutor was furious. The judge seemed to side with the prosecutor, telling Reilly, "The witness already identified the trophy. I see no need that he has to identify each one individually." He overruled the objection of the public defender.

The prosecutor presented pictures of the Ford sedan with a license plate hanging by one bolt along with the report of the theft of the same vehicle and a subsequent stolen license report. Then he brought out the 22-caliber pistol that was found hidden behind a drawer in the defendant's apartment.

During questioning by the prosecutor, Billy admitted that he was driving a stolen vehicle but that he didn't steal it.

"I paid somebody I met at a bar 50 bucks a week to use it until the license plate expired; then the guy from the bar disappeared. I figured he stole it but I wrecked my car drinking too much and needed a car. The license plate had expired, so I stole the license plate off some car in a parking lot."

He then admitted that he entered the house on Monk Road through an open window and exited through a rear door.

"I believe we have shown probable cause, your honor," said the prosecutor.

The public defender asked Billy about the gun found in his house. Billy swore as he had to Reilly previously, that he never owned a gun in his life and never wanted to own one.

"I did steal a lot of silver from the house but that's all. There was nobody there. I didn't shoot nobody. I wouldn't shoot an animal. That ain't my gun. I swear to God!"

Billy Thompson was told he could step down, that at this time there are no further questions. However, the public defender asked Detective Theo Harrison to take the witness stand. After Harrison was sworn in, Reilly asked the detective if he found the gun when he went through the kitchen the first time.

"I did not."

"So Detective, to understand this correctly you will have been doing this for 20 years short of just a few months when you retire. Correct?"

"Correct."

"And you are a very experienced homicide detective, yet for some reason, going through every single drawer cabinet sofa you found nothing but when the second officer who assisted you with the search warrant inspected that same area minutes after you did, he found the gun that you claim belonged to the defendant William Thompson. Is that correct?"

"Correct." Harrison sounded somber.

"Detective Harrison. Whose name did you find the pistol registered to?"

"The serial numbers were filed down and we were not able to determine that."

"Detective, did ballistics do a match of the bullet that killed Mrs. Moore with the pistol that you claim belongs to the defendant?"

"No. They were unable to confirm because the inside of the rifling had been roughed up with some kind of a boring tool similar to what is used to clean out shotguns."

"Detective Harrison are you aware that there are nearly 4,000,000 22-caliber pistols in the United States ?"

"I never checked. Never had any reason to."

"Counselors." The judge brought down his gavel. I find more than sufficient reason to show probable cause."

***

Over the next several days Marcus Reilly was unable to sleep. He actually believed his clients and felt that they were being railroaded; however, the evidence showed otherwise. He went back to the Montgomery County correctional facility to go over step-by-step everything that happened the night the two had claimed that Billy burglarized the home.

Without an address but knowing that his clients were pulled over him within a mile from the premises, Marcus drove the mile back from the point that they were apprehended, writing down each and every address. He then spent several hours going door-to-door to interview the residents. When he approached Hampton Court he had to use the phone box to call for someone to permit him to enter. Then a bell rang in his head. He thought that neither Billy nor Albert ever mentioned that they would have to go through a gate. That was strange. So many conversations and not one time did either of them ever mention that there was a powered gate that needed a code.

He went to the next six adjoining properties finding one person who told them that their neighbors, Sam and Mary Johnson were vacationing at their home on the French Riviera but were coming home the end of that week.

He planned to return and took down the address. He approached the home and found there was no gate whatsoever. He left his business card in their mailbox with a note to please call on an urgent matter.

The following evening he went back to the few bars that Billy frequented hoping to get some better insight on Billy and his personality.

At Tiny Tim's Bar, he ordered scotch on the rocks just to get comfortable with the surrounding people at the bar.

"Do any of you guys here know Billy Thompson? I'm not the law. I'm here to help him and I need some input from you guys."

Besides some grunts and groans, mostly everybody had something good to say about him including a six-foot-four curly-haired 30-year-old with tattoos up and down his arms and a snake tattoo around his neck.

"Billy fell off the barstool," he said pointing down the bar. "He landed on his wrist and broke it but wanted to drive home. I told him, 'No way. you're plastered and you got to go to the hospital.' He gave me some shit but he's a little tiny guy so I pushed him in my car and drove him to the hospital emergency. We waited there about an hour because they were busy with two people's gunshot wounds and after they x-rayed him they put him in a plaster cast because he broke his wrist."

"Do you remember when that was?" Reilly asked.

"Naw. Sometime in December. I know it just started to snow but nothing much came down overnight maybe an inch."

Reilly then called the local television station informing them that he's doing an investigation and just needs to know what day in December there an accumulation of one inch of snow. He was transferred to someone in the weather department and they provided him with two dates. One where there was a maximum of one-inch accumulation in Philadelphia and another day when there were four inches. However, on the day of the four-inch snowfall, the snow started at 10 a.m. and stopped at approximately 4 p.m.

With that information, public defender Reilly headed to the Episcopal hospital to see if they had a record of a patient in the emergency room named William Thompson on that same day. A very courteous nurse behind the counter found his chart which showed that he entered the hospital's emergency ward signing in at 11:12 p.m. complaining about his pains in his right wrist and was x-rayed at 12:45 a.m. At 2:30-3:10 a.m. Dr. Cooper placed his right wrist and hand in a plaster cast with instructions to return in two weeks for it to be removed and replaced with a removable one. At approximately 4:30 a.m. he was given one Percocet and discharged with a prescription for 12 more for pain if needed.

"I see there was a note that someone brought William Thompson here and who also drove him home since he would not be released in his condition," the nurse said. "He obviously was in no condition to drive especially after taking the Percocet."

Marcus wanted to kiss her. "Thank you so much. You might have just saved someone's life."

Now Reilly was totally convinced that Billy Thompson was telling him the truth and he felt certain that Detective Harrison was setting him up. And he had actual facts that Billy Thompson was at a bar, fell off the stool, and broke his right wrist the night that Mrs. Jacqueline Phyllis Moore was murdered. He was treated in the hospital and not released till 4:30 a.m. in no condition to drive and was escorted home by some good Samaritan from Tiny Tim's bar.

Reilly had obtained a copy of the medical examiner's report which stated that time of death occurred between 10:30 p.m. and 1:30 a.m.

Giving the Johnsons on Monk Road one day to settle back in their home after returning from the French Riviera, Reilly drove there at 11 o'clock that morning. They still had a mountain of suitcases piled in their entranceway, a few of them opened.

He questioned them about articles stolen from a room on the right side of their house and was surprised to find that they seldom used that room except to store articles to give to local charity auctions. They walked him to the room and were surprised to see the disarray and items missing, including the trophy that Mr. Rodney Moore gave to Mr. Johnson as a joke.

They were both glad that there was no damage done to the house nor any of their valuable items stolen; however, they each blamed the other for leaving a window unlocked.

Reilly assured both Mr. and Mrs. Johnson that all the items would be returned shortly following the disposition of this case. He told them the heart-wrenching story of Billy's abuse as a youngster and how it affected him.

"He's no angel, I guarantee you that, but his life is going to change and I'm going to be sure of it."

"They can keep those things especially Rodney's golf trophy. He pissed me off every Saturday when we went golfing. He won every single time, three years in a row, and one day about four years ago he came over with the trophy and a bottle of bourbon to tell me that the last time we played he cheated. We were the best of friends."

Marcus Reilly left then placed a call to the local newspaper asking for a reporter who might have some background information on District Attorney Dennis Mazur and Detective Theo Harrison. He was informed that the previous summer, the Society Section featured a family gathering and a photo of Dennis Mazur's arm around his cousin, Detective Theo Harrison.

Chapter 23

Reilly organized his notes in sequential order then placed a call to Theo Harrison.

"This is Detective Harrison can I help you?"

"Detective, the question should be can you help me. You see detective, I now have confirmed everything that you have done and can show, not only your utter incompetence but also prove that you criminally planted the 22-caliber pistol which you illegally removed from the evidence locker. At 4 o'clock this afternoon I want your ass and your cousin Harold's in my office. No fucking excuses. You both be there and don't you dare be late!

"If you are, then I'm out of the picture and my cousin will lead a team FBI agents to audit the evidence locker and arrest you. At the same time, all the TV and media will be there. One last thing Theo, if you are late you can say goodbye to your pension." A smiling Marcus C. Reilly hung up.

***

At 3:30 p.m. a meek detective Harrison appeared at his office and five minutes later his cousin, District Attorney

Dennis Mazur, arrived. Reilly's secretary brought them into the conference room. Seated at the head of the table was Marcus and behind him on the wall was a 3-foot photograph of a Federal Superior Court Justice with his arm around Marcus. The two seated at the table looked above Marcus's head staring at the photograph.

Reilly noticed them looking. "That's my uncle. He's been a superior court justice for ten years and my inspiration. I clerked for him when I graduated law school.

"Gentlemen, I'm not looking to be a thorn in any one's side. If anything, I'm trying to find a good way out so neither of you are embarrassed or possibly be facing criminal charges. First of all, Billy Thompson was in the hospital the night of Mrs. Moore's murder. I have spoken with the doctor and a nurse at Episcopal hospital and after they were shown his records, they confirmed it. I have a written statement from the person that brought him to the hospital and brought him back to his apartment hours after the homicide. Secondly, Hampton court, the residence of the former Mrs. Jacqueline Phyllis Moore, was not robbed. The articles that were found in the trunk of the vehicle that my clients were driving came from a home three doors up belonging to the Johnsons. They were good friends of the Moores. Four years ago, Rodney Moore personally gave his golfing trophy to his buddy Mr. Johnson.

"Theo, for some reason or other you never notified me or the court that you received a call from the Philadelphia Police Department informing you that they had no interest in William Thompson because the warrant was issued incorrectly and withdrawn. Yet you use that as additional evidence in the hearing to show cause." He continued, "Then you, Theo, entered the evidence room on the pretense of leaving the search warrant there and then walked out with a 22-caliber pistol that had serial numbers on it. That pistol had remained in the evidence room for the past six months from another case. You removed the serial numbers from the pistol and bored out the barrel and then hid it in the drawer of Billy Thompson's apartment, pretending to let the Philadelphia officer think that he found it. The police officer knew that you placed it there because he saw you do it from the other room. So now here we are. We have a person and his friend that you have ridiculed and accused of first-degree murder. You both conspired to have these charges brought against these victims. Now, what do we do?"

The room was silent. Both representatives of the law were speechless. Then Mazur asked, "What would you suggest?"

Reilly responded, "There is an easy way out of this, causing no harm and possibly keeping your pension. First Mazur, I want you to drop all charges against both my clients. Whatever excuse you come up with that's OK with me. As far as the burglary which Billy Thompson admitted to the Johnsons—after being told what he was put through—decided that they are not even going to report a burglary, especially since those items were going to be given to a charity.

"We all now know that of Mrs. Moore's murderer is out there. I want you guys to do everything possible to find that murderer. Legally. In the name of my uncle the superior court justice. I demand that you do it legally.

"As far as Billy Thompson driving a stolen vehicle, which it turns out, he did not steal but affixed a stolen license plate, I would suggest that we come together on a plea bargain. He will admit that he drove a vehicle that turned out to be stolen and steal the license plate. I want you to suggest a one-year sentence with two years' probation. And both my clients should be eligible for release after six months minus the one month that they have spent so far in jail.

"Are we all in agreement gentlemen?"

A very shaky district attorney confirmed.

"I will write up the papers tomorrow to that effect and present it to the court."

Marcus C Reilly proudly stood up and looked at his uncle's picture on the wall while holding back a smile. "Gentlemen. Let's all get on with our lives and thank you for your cooperation."

***

Newspaper and television reporters covered news conference at which District Attorney Dennis Mazur praised the efforts of Detective Theo Harrison, who made certain that even the accused are treated fairly. Through his diligent work and that of his staff they were able to discover new evidence that proves neither of the accused William Thompson nor Albert Young Jr. had anything to do with the homicide of Mrs. J.P Moore, Mazur told them. He informed the press that they are following other leads in the investigation.

Then the district attorney thanked everyone for attending and refused to take any questions. Both he and Detective Harrison went their respective ways.

***

Upon returning to his office Harrison found Detective Simpson going through his case file notes. Picking up the phone he told Harrison that he is trying to reach Joanne Lawrence the physical therapist.

"You did a background check on her before and found that she was living was a drug dealer. Did you just drop it?" Harrison asked.

"No, I did not. I met with her at her apartment and questioned her thoroughly; it's all in the report. She never had a pistol. The two times that she was arrested she was released with no charges. She was only arrested because she was living with that Chaz Galloni, the drug dealer. Theo, I don't understand. You told me to drop everything; that the two burglars were the ones that killed Mrs. Moore. It was no sense following any further. Besides, there's nothing that links her at all, plus both Lawrence and her boyfriend had good alibis that we checked out. What else is there to check?"

"Well let's get into that file deeper and don't drop the ball since everybody's got their eyes on this case."

Simpson was a bit pissed. As soon as Harrison left Simpson's cubicle Simpson realized that he never checked out Victor thoroughly, nor a Rico Rodriguez who Victor fought with and now was supposedly now living in Trenton.

155

He also noticed that he never got back in touch with the housekeeper, who was supposed to get him information about her boyfriend Aleksander. He dreaded that, since it was so difficult to understand anything that she said.

He spent over an hour on the phone trying to track the whereabouts of Rico Rodriguez in Trenton. The local police weren't cooperative, as well as and a detective who complained that he had more than enough problems on his hands to look for anybody.

"We have Puerto Ricans fighting Guatemalans. Blacks fighting both. This area turned into a hell hole I don't have time to track somebody down for you."

After hearing that response from the disgruntled detective, Simpson was very happy being a detective in Lower Marion. He planned to take a dreaded drive to Trenton.

The following morning after checking in, he took his file with him and drove the expressway to the interstate heading into New Jersey. One hour later he came to an address that was in a complaint associated with Rodriguez.

The entire area looked very similar to some areas in Chester. It seemed to him that there were hundreds of homes squeezed together on every city block. Finding the address, he walked up three steps and knocked on the door. A minute later a 16-year-old boy opened the door.

"What choo want? Ain't nobody here."

Then someone from the rear of the house yelled, "Somebody looking for Rico?"

The detective knew that this was a typical response from anybody who thought that the police meant trouble.

"I'm only here to ask him some questions. It's about his friend Victor."

Then a large Hispanic man came to the front door and identified himself as Jose, Rico's brother-in-law.

"Victor is no friend of Rico's and besides Rico hasn't been here since he got involved with that bad dude in Chester."

"I heard that they both fought over money from a deal that went bad." Simpson was testing him.

"That's right." Jose continued, "Rico and Victor were buying this guy's taxicab in Chester real cheap. They was going to be partners and be legit. Rico knew this guy who was going back to Puerto Rico and he had a taxicab with a license for sale. He had to sell it quickly to get the money for his family and he told Rico that it was worth $25-$35,000 but he would take $10,000 quickly instead of using one of those brokers that take a big share and maybe never sell it.

"When Rico gave the guy the $10,000, the guy gave him the taxi and the title and told him he'll bring the taxi license papers over the next day to get transferred at the State. Next day the dude never showed. Rico and Victor wound up with a car that was worthless and Victor wanted his $5000 back that he gave Rico. That's what they was fighting about."

"So you're telling me that they both got defrauded out of $10,000."

Detective Simpson then thanked the man and handed him his card requesting that he have Rico call him since there might be a warrant for him which he would rather not see happen. Simpson wanted to put a little fear into this man even though there was no warrant.

After taking notes, Simpson headed back to the office to report to Harrison. When he arrived at the office Harrison was on the phone talking to Robert Snyder. Simpson wrote a quick note asking Harrison to hand him the phone when he's done talking to Snyder.

"I don't know what to tell you, Mr. Snyder. There's nobody more disappointed than all of us here. Everything fell into place and then we checked to make sure everything was perfect for a trial and we found out overwhelming proof that neither of those two that we had in custody were involved in any way with the murder of Mrs. Moore nor did they steal anything out of the house."

"But Detective, I identified the trophy as belonging to Mr. Rodney Moore. How do you explain that?" Snyder asked.

"It seems as though Mr. Moore and Sam Johnson were golfing buddies. For over three years Mr. Moore supposedly won almost every round that they played and as a joke, Mr.

Moore gave his buddy Johnson the trophy on his birthday. It did not come from Hampton Court it came from the Johnson home up the road. Mr. Snyder that's why none of the other objects looked familiar to you."

"I understand, Detective. It's just very disappointing. Thinking one day you have the murderers in hand and the next day nothing. Back to step one. Is there anything that I can help with? I'm starting back to law school soon and won't be as available."

"Mr. Snyder, I realize you're disappointed. As I said we all are." Harrison was glad that he didn't have to answer any other questions. "If anything comes up I will leave a message on your answering machine. Hold on, Detective Simpson has a question for you."

"Sorry to bother you, Mr. Snyder, but is there anything that you can tell me about Stasha's boyfriend Aleksander?"

"Only that about every week or so he'd be there to drop her off to work and then later in the day he would return to pick her up."

"Did you ever meet him?"

"I really never paid much attention, but one time I saw this burly, seedy-looking character removing something from the trunk of his car, which I assumed was some of Stasha's cleaning materials, and that morning I saw her with a black eye. I asked her what happened and she said, 'No. No. No.' So I just dropped it. I didn't think she bumped her head on the door. But that wasn't my business."

Simpson continued, "I interviewed Stasha with great difficulty. Can you give me her phone number? I just want to get Aleksander's last name and information."

"I may have the address book in my car. When I get in I'll call you."

As soon as Robert hung up the phone, it rang. It was Amanda calling to tell him she just heard the on the news that additional information just received proved that the two suspects that were being held for trial were innocent. She tried to console Robert that eventually, they'll find the murderer. She asked him about staying over for the weekend and he was glad to accept the invitation.

***

Going through the mind of Detective Harrison was the question of who benefited from the attempted burglary that led to the murder? His mind flashed to Robert. Was Robert being too cooperative in calling several times a week? It was a simple thing to do. Was he doing this to see if we were on a trail that would possibly lead to him? Why did Robert tell me that he was the sole beneficiary? Was it because he knew he would look bad if we found out first? Being that he was the sole beneficiary, he would have access to the safe deposit box which every person of means would have. What could have been in there? Did he notify the IRS about the safe deposit box? He was there at the house the night that the murder took place. He told us that he was sleeping in his apartment but was he? He seemed upset but he was also an actor. I baited him by letting him think that we traced his name and found records that he owned a 22-caliber pistol. He didn't realize that without us having the serial number of the pistol it would be impossible to check. The NRA made sure that there was not a public registry. He then admitted that he owned a 22-caliber pistol that he supposedly sold to a pawnshop for $25. Could he still have it? Could that pistol be the one that killed Mrs. Moore?

"Theo. Have time to talk?" Detective Simpson asked.
"I want to brew a fresh pot of coffee. Do you want some also? Then I'm all yours." They walked to the small backroom office that was used as a conference room.

As the coffee was brewing, Simpson went over what he had on Victor and Rico Rodriguez. He explained about the business deal with somebody Rico knew who was selling their taxicab and taxi license for $10,000 and how both of them were going to run a legit business. Victor wound up getting screwed, and supposedly so did Rico, but Victor felt all along that he was set up. They had an argument that turned into a fight and then Rico agreed to give Victor $2500, supposedly out of his pocket.

159

After Simpson spoke with Victor he realized that the $2500 went towards his security deposit to rent the apartment. As far as Simpson was concerned, neither of them had anything to do with anything at Hampton Court.

Harrison went over all of the thoughts that he had about Robert Snyder. Some things just did not add up. He asked Simpson to get in touch with Robert Snyder and ask him when he purchased the pistol and the name of the store that he purchased it from. Then the name of the pawnshop where he supposedly sold it.

"According to the law, storekeepers are supposed to keep records of all gun sales for a period of 20 years. It's a bitch trying to search them, since they're all handwritten records and usually kept in the storage room. But let's start somewhere," Harrison instructed Simpson.

***

"The word in our office is that one of the detectives planted the supposed murder weapon in the apartment of one of the burglars," Amanda told Robert.

"I can't believe it. I met with both detectives numerous times since it happened and I am shocked that they would do anything like that."

"Bobby, it happens all too often. Most of the time, it's one detective or officer trying to help another out of a jam which might've been a bad judgment by an officer, especially when it comes to a shooting. Now the pressure is on them even more to find out who killed her. They will. It may take time but they will find out."

"Do you want to take a shower with me?" asked Amanda. "It will get your mind off everything else and on me."

"My mind is always on you and my eyes would enjoy taking a shower with you."

Chapter 24

The following morning at breakfast Amanda mentioned to Robert that detective Harrison was somewhat put off with her when she inquired about activity with the case.

"He seemed fixated on you. My concern is that he continues that course and doesn't see the forest for the trees."

Sitting in the living room, he called his answering machine to check for messages. One message was from the admissions secretary at Temple University giving him the starting date for his class. The other was from Detective Simpson.

"Mr. Snyder. Just looking back over our notes I wanted to know if you remember the date when and the gun shop where you purchased your 22-caliber pistol? Also the name of the pawnshop that you sold it to. I realize that was several years back but I could use your assistance. We're just trying to fill in all the blanks. You have my card with my phone number. I'll await your call."

"You must have ESP," Robert joked to Amanda. "I just checked with the answering machine and there was a message from Detective Simpson requesting information about a 22-caliber pistol that I bought years ago in Philadelphia. He also wanted the name of the pawnshop that I sold it to. How do I ever find a date that I bought about ten years ago? Not only that, but a while back they asked me what I did with my 22-caliber pistol. If they knew that I owned one then they would have the information. Wouldn't they?"

"Bobby, they probably just baited you when they asked about your pistol before. All sales records of handguns are required to be held for 20 years. But there is no way that they could know that you owned one unless they had the serial number and the vendor who sold it to you. It seems like their prior fixation is back on you. Don't pay attention to it. They finally are doing their job."

***

"This is Detective Simpson. Can I help you?"

"This is Robert Snyder returning your call."

"Glad you called, Mr. Snyder. Were you able to find any information for me?"

Robert gave the detective all the information that he could think of. "Ruttenberg's in Philadelphia. Frankly, I thought you had that information when you asked me about the gun before. As for the date, I don't remember but it was around the time when Nixon resigned if that helps. The pawnshop was on Samson Street about one block east of Broad Street. There's no way that I'd be able to find my receipt for it. I would not even know where to look."

"Thank you so much. I appreciate getting back to me so soon. If I have any more questions I'll get back to you."

As soon as Simpson hung up he looked in the phone directory for Ruttenberg's Gun Shop. It was easy to find in the Yellow Pages since they had a full-page ad. He called and asked for the manager or owner and identified himself. An assistant manager picked up the phone and informed Simpson that he did not have access to any of the records of sales beyond four years ago and he's not authorized to open up their storage unit in the industrial park where old records are kept.

"This is very urgent. It involves a murder investigation and I insist that you reach either the owner or someone above you to get me access to where those records are stored."

"Detective. Give me a phone number where I can have the owner reach you. I'll be talking to him in the morning and stress the urgency. We certainly wish to cooperate with all law-enforcement officials, especially when it involves an investigation. You will find everyone here cooperative."

Simpson reported to Harrison and told him that he felt that Robert Snyder was being honest but that he also realized that Snyder was a self-professed actor albeit a non-successful one.

"When somebody wealthy like Mrs. Moore dies there's no chance that she didn't have a safe deposit box. I want you to find out where it is or where it was and when it was last accessed," Detective Harrison instructed.

That was not an easy task. Simpson had no way of telling which bank she did business with but figured the easiest thing is just to ask Robert Snyder, who, among other things, was her personal secretary. By this time Simpson was in no mood to call back Robert Snyder. The first thing on his mind was getting to the records to find the gun that Robert owned.

***

The next morning while Simpson was sitting at his desk having his usual coffee, he received a call from Mr. Sam Ruttenberg, the gun store owner. Mr. Ruttenberg explained that the records are stored in an industrial park storage unit that they have leased for the past 15 years. He explained that there were countless boxes of sales records and he would be glad to make them available to him but he warned Simpson that it would be like finding a needle in a haystack. Simpson then explained that he knew the week when the gun was supposedly purchased, which was a big help to the owner. However, Simpson would have to go through all the records himself.

"We had a flood here a few years back when this area got hit with four inches of rain and it took five people to pull all the boxes out of storage and dry off the papers, including sales and purchase records. Just be prepared detective, since nothing was put back in chronological order. As papers dried out, they were put into the closest dry cardboard box. When would you like to come down so I can make arrangements with one of my employees to open up the unit? He will also have to close it when you're done," a very cooperative Mr. Ruttenberg said.

"I'm going to check my schedule and see when I can come down for the day. I'll get back to you Mr. Ruttenberg. Thank you. I know this is an inconvenience."

Reluctantly, Simpson placed another call to Robert Snyder's answering machine inquiring as to what bank or banks that Mrs. Moore did business with and where she had her safe deposit box.

Robert had not interrupted his amorous weekend with his bride-to-be to check his messages. Being with Amanda was more important than anything else.

Monday morning came and after Robert enjoyed a spinach omelet that Amanda made, he retrieved messages on his answering machine hearing only one, yet again from Detective Simpson. He called and Simpson answered after being paged.

"I wish to apologize, Mr. Snyder, for bothering you again but I just need your help. Do you know in which bank or banks Mrs. Moore kept her safe deposit box?"

"Mrs. Moore had two checking accounts that I'm aware of and one credit card. I was never privy to a safe deposit box. None of my duties would've included that. The one account that I wrote checks out of was Gladwyn Bank and Trust. She had another personal checking account that was not under my watch and that was with PennCo Bank. I'm sure that you can check with them about any safe deposit box or boxes. Is there anything else detective?" Robert answered somewhat sarcastically.

"I appreciate your cooperation and, again, I'm sorry if I'm bothering you."

Robert planned to go to Temple University Law School's admissions office and get a list of the books that he needed for classes.

***

Simpson called Ruttenberg's and made arrangements to meet an employee at the industrial park in South Philadelphia for 10 o'clock Tuesday morning.

He was there promptly at 10 a.m. and met with Charles, a security guard in Ruttenberg's employ.

Charles opened up the steel overhead roll-up garage door even though there was an access door. "The lighting is in here is terrible. That's why I opened up the garage door to get natural daylight in for you. They have never been able to get that damp smell out of this building as many times as they tried. It kills my allergies because of the mold. We had two companies here to get rid of the mold and both told us that everything had to be brought outside and aired out for a few days. We can't do that. So we put up with the mold."

What Simpson saw in front of him was the huge storage locker that went about 30 feet deep and 15 feet wide. Storage boxes of cardboard 18 inches wide by about 24 inches deep stacked one on top of each other covering all the walls almost reaching the ceiling and three rows deep. It looked like a storage vault for the national public records. He wondered how anyone could ever find anything in this room.

"Charles, can you point me in the direction of 1974 July and August?"

"Detective, all I can say is good luck. I don't know if Mr. Ruttenberg told you but a few years back there was a flood in here and all the employees that they could get were moving all the boxes out. Rain had broken through the ceiling. There were several inches of water on the floor saturating all the boxes. They put all the papers that had purchases and sales in new boxes but plenty of the papers were soaked through. Nobody cared since these records were just being stored and that's the only time anyone ever came here. You are the first visitor looking for something. I would just say start at one side and see what you can."

A very disappointed Simpson just shook his head. He understood what he had in front of him. The security guard had to remain there with him but could stay outside away from the smell of mold. Simpson took on the battle. He took a Polaroid camera and photographed all the stacks from different directions using two rolls of film. He thought he'd mark an "X" each box after he went through the papers inside. Identifying the content within each box was difficult since most of them had no new labels affixed when they were salvaging the records. The first box he opened was an indication of the problem he was facing. There were records that had nothing to do with the sale of handguns but for articles purchased from army surplus. And several of those were distorted from being water-soaked.

He went back to his car and took out another roll of Polaroid film. Then he took just one photo of the inside contents that he laid on the floor. After putting everything back in the carton he put an X on the box.

Three hours later still not finding July or August 1974, he took a break and went to lunch even asking Charles if he'd like to join him. Charles agreed and closed the garage door and went with Simpson to the Melrose Diner in South Philly where they could always get a good wholesome meal.

Sitting in the booth Charles noticed that Simpson was rubbing his eyes.

"Detective. I think the dampness has gotten to you. I see you rubbing your eyes."

"Yeah. You're right. I'm going to have to pull some people in the office to assist me. This is just too much. I could be here a year," a disgusted Simpson replied.

After a very enjoyable lunch, Simpson dropped Charles off at the industrial park and headed to his office. His eyes did not stop itching. An hour later when he entered the headquarters, he went right to the men's room and washed his hands and face then looked around for the first aid kit where he found eyewash solution. Five minutes later the discomfort left his eyes and he laid out the photos on Harrison's desk.

"What's this?" he asked Simpson.

"Theo, I can't do this alone. I don't even know if I can do this with a half a dozen people. The place stinks from mold, which was killing my eyes, and I only got through a half a dozen cartons. There are hundreds there as you can see in these photos and nothing is organized."

"Take a break and see what other day you can go there and try to find out if you can get some volunteers. We need evidence of that pistol."

Simpson spent the next hour going over other cases that he was working on which he did not want to neglect but his instructions were to lay heavy on the homicide of Mrs. Moore. He then called Gladwyn Bank and Trust identifying himself and requesting information about a safe deposit box in the name of this Mrs. Jacqueline Phyliss Moore. His request was denied since they did not know who he was and it was against their privacy rules. He insisted, explaining that it was integral to the murder investigation. He was told by the bank manager to bring in a letter of authorization and he will make the records available.

Detective Harrison called his cousin Harold Mazur and asked him to call the bank manager. At 3 o'clock the manager brought Simpson to the filing cabinet and found the safe deposit box number for Mrs. Moore.

"Can I see inside?" Simpson asked.

The manager explained that he would need the key or else the box would have to be drilled open and they would need a court order to do so. "Why not call the executor of the estate?"

"That's Robert Snyder," Simpson said.

"Hmmm. I don't see a Robert Snyder authorized on the account; only Mrs. Moore and her executor, William Spaulding Esquire."

Then he showed Simpson the signature card. The detective saw that the last person to enter the box was William Spaulding. Just one day after Mrs. Moore's death.

A very courteous Simpson requested that the manager photocopy the signature card showing when the box was opened and closed and thanked him. As he was leaving he said to the manager, "How is it that William Spaulding was given access to the safe deposit box after the death of Mrs. Moore? You realize that after the death of a safe deposit box owner the bank is supposed to seal that box until it is authorized to be opened."

The manager was speechless.

"We know that Mr. Spaulding is the executor and he said he needed access to see if there's anything of importance in it. Knowing him for so many years and his law firm we felt it was all right."

"Did he leave with anything?"

"I have no idea, Detective. I just assumed he was doing his job and we paid no attention as we're not supposed to. He was given access to a private room as all of our customers are."

"Thank you."

Simpson left and returned to his office where he made an appointment to meet with William Spaulding for 11 a.m. the following day.

Chapter 25

Robert kept his appointment with admissions at Temple School of Law, paid his enrollment then went to the bookstore and purchased everything on the list of items for his classes.

Without realizing it Robert was spending more and more time with Amanda at her townhouse and enjoying being with her and was seldom at his apartment.

The evening after Simpson had called inquiring about the safe deposit box, Amanda had a question.

"Since you were the sole beneficiary of the estate you should have been given the keys and authority for the safe deposit box. It was in the will. I wonder why you were never informed about it?"

"Maybe she didn't have one?"

"Bobby. It's inconceivable that anyone with financial wealth would not have a safe deposit box to hold important documents or simply to hold sentimental documents. It's also a great place to leave your jewelry if you're going away."

"Mrs. Moore never mentioned anything about a safe deposit box; she told me so many things in total confidence because of the relationship that we had. I think if she had one and there was anything of importance in there she would've told me. After all, she knew that I was the sole beneficiary although I never knew."

"You know me , working in the DA's office I never stop asking questions but I think you're probably right. I'll place a call tomorrow to Simpson or his boss Harrison anyway, to find out if they discovered anything."

On the following morning, Simpson was at the office of Calhoun, Spaulding, and Fiengold for his 11 o'clock appointment with William Spaulding.

"Good to see you, Detective Simpson. I saw the news that the murder suspects turned out to be innocent. That must've been a heartbreaker when you believe that there's an ironclad case and something blows it apart."

"It was definitely disappointing. Every single thing seemed to point to Billy Thompson, but we're still at it. I came here came today just for a bit of help. Can you tell me anything about Mrs. Moore's safe deposit box or boxes?"

"Please explain yourself. I don't understand what your question is," Spaulding said.

"Well, what I don't understand is why you were at Gladwyn Bank and Trust and accessing Mrs. Moore's safe deposit box. That seems unusual."

"Detective. I find it a straight matter of a fact. Nothing unusual at all. That's part of my job as executor of the estate."

"But counselor, you were there a day after she was murdered and you know the law. After her death, the bank should have sealed the safe deposit box but they didn't. What was there that you removed without being in the presence of the State Taxing Authority or a letter from the court? From what I understand the process alone could take 30 days if not longer."

"Detective Simpson. My first concern and duty has always been for the well-being of Mrs. Moore. I was appointed by her to be the executor of her estate. I had every right to check and see what, if anything, was in the safe deposit box that would be due to Robert Snyder, the sole beneficiary of everything that she had."

"And what was it that you removed from the safe deposit box?" Simpson inquired.

"Surprisingly, nothing. The safe deposit box was empty. Clean as could be. Not a piece of jewelry nor any documents." Spaulding continued, "If I found anything I would have presented it to Robert Snyder, the sole beneficiary."

"One last thing, Mr. Spaulding. Can you tell me if there's anything that you might know about Robert Snyder's owning a gun?"

"That little peashooter that he used to keep under his pillow? He probably still does. He was paranoid sharing an apartment with a couple other unemployed actors."

"You know nothing about him selling the pistol to a pawnshop?

"I doubt that he would do such a thing. He really was paranoid and it became a habit."

"Counselor, if you think of something that just doesn't seem right to you about Robert, you know, a twinge in your stomach, please call me."

"Detective, I recommended him to Mrs. Moore and she thought highly of him. Obviously she did feel for him because it was her desire to leave everything to him. With her permission, I actually tape-recorded the session about her estate planning which was her will. You know she had no close relatives and a couple of nephews or nieces who never ever called or cared about her. If I thought that there was something to implicate Robert or even a question about his integrity I would be the first to call you."

Then Bill Spaulding reached across his desk and extended his hand to shake Simpson's The meeting was over.

***

As soon as Amanda finished her lunch, she had to attend a meeting scheduled for 1:15 p.m. in City Hall. She returned at 2:30 and placed a call to Detective Simpson. Finding he was out of the office, she asked for detective Harrison who picked up the phone.

171

"Harrison. Can I help you? "

"Hi, Detective. This is Amanda Dillington. We've spoken before. Is there anything that you can tell me as an update since the charges were dropped against Thompson and Young?"

"The only thing I can tell you in confidence is that we are checking the records from Ruttenberg's in Philly to check on the pistol that Robert claims he purchased from them. I've just given Detective Simpson two young officers to go through cartons of sales and purchase orders using the approximate date that Robert provided. We need to find that pistol."

"I certainly can understand, Detective, and I hope you don't mind if I contact you occasionally for updates." Amanda hung up.

***

When Simpson returned to the office after his meeting with Bill Spaulding he brought Harrison up to date. He also mentioned that Robert was paranoid and for years slept with his 22-caliber pistol under his pillow even after he moved away from a couple of sleazy characters that he shared an apartment with. He also thought that Snyder would never pawn the pistol. Harrison told Simpson that he was able to find two rookies that would work with him for two days if needed going through Ruttenberg's records.

"If they can meet me here early in the morning the three of us will go down in one car," Simpson said.

He then arranged to meet the security guard at Ruttenberg's storage locker. Before leaving in the morning he would take a Benadryl allergy pill.

***

First thing the next morning he met with the two rookies and headed to South Philadelphia encountering typical traffic jams. When he arrived at the industrial park he turned to the third set of buildings where he met Charles, the security guard for Ruttenberg's. As soon as Charles saw Simpson with two other policemen he opened up the overhead door.

The smell of dampness and mold permeated the air as soon as they approached the storage unit. Simpson was glad that he had taken a Benadryl at 7 o'clock that morning. He had a plan. Using the Polaroid photographs that he had taken, he instructed the two rookies to take one wall of the cartons using the ladder and to hand down each carton one at a time trying to figure out how, if ever, the cartons were organized. When each carton was brought to the floor a quick look through each one was ordered by Simpson to see what dates were on receipts and invoices. This, he hoped, would narrow down the dates of the contents without inspecting every single paper held within the boxes. As each vertical row was gone through, he instructed the rookies to replace them in the same order in the event he had to double-check. After two hours Simpson was getting dejected since only a few of the cartons were organized with receipts and purchases from the same year. This time he took a break with both rookies and Charles; the four went for lunch once again at the Melrose Diner.

After a 30-minute lunch, they headed back to continue their work. Simpson scanned through various pages after the officer on the ground was doing a cursory inspection to see if they were organized by year and then hopefully by the month.

At 3:55 p.m. on the first day the younger of the two rookies who inspected the contents called Simpson's attention to what a box with the year and the month they were seeking. There it was: August 1974. Now to dissect every page without forgetting where the file came from in the event they had to look at the cartons before and after it.

"I have it, Detective Simpson," the elated rookie shouted. "Take a look. It's a sale of a Colt Junior, 22-caliber short semi-automatic pistol serial number 59711CC to Robert Snyder on August 9th, 1974."

"Let me get the Polaroid to photograph the box and the file jacket. You guys did a good job. I'm proud of you. You made my day much easier," Simpson complimented both of them.

Moments later they all were working to replace the cartons that they took down so everything was the same as when they first arrived, except for removing one folder that had the purchase by Robert Snyder.

Back at the office, Simpson found that Theo had already gone home. It was after 6 p.m. He didn't want to call Theo at home but was anxious to report what he felt was great news.

***

The next morning when Harrison arrived, sitting on his desk was the bill of sale from Ruttenberg's to Robert Snyder. A jubilant Harrison went over to the Simpson's cubicle finding him on the phone. Harrison put his arm around Simpson's back and squeezed without saying anything. When Simpson finished his phone call he walked over to Harrison's desk looking somewhat dejected.

"What's wrong with you? I thought you'd be tap dancing finding this record, a real needle in a haystack?"

"Theo, I placed a call to the National Tracing Center in Martinsburg West Virginia wanting to find out if this pistol might've been used in another homicide and was shocked to find out that they have no true database; everything is done by hand having numerous people searching through thousands upon thousands of records."

"You can thank the NRA for that," Harrison said. "They protested any national database so we're living in the 19th century as far as I'm concerned when it comes to records pertaining to handguns. I don't care about any other homicide, just this one. Did you find the pawnshop that he supposedly sold the gun to?"

"Not yet. Just finished finding the records in that stinkpot building."

"Track down the pawnshop. Hopefully, they have a record of the purchase and the sale. I would not be surprised if they act ignorant because so many of them are sleazy; they'll sell anything to make a dollar. Most of them will buy stolen merchandise and act ignorant when they're caught. We do need to find that gun," Harrison instructed.

Driving the streets of Philadelphia, Simpson went up and back on Samson Street both East and West of Broad St., to no avail. He could not find any pawnshop. He thought that with the building revival going on in Center City, perhaps one of the new buildings was where the previous pawnshop was if there was a previous pawnshop. He parked his vehicle and went door-to-door on both sides of the street inquiring from shopkeepers if they knew where there was a pawnshop previously. He was told that there was one that is now a record shop and that the pawnshop closed about three years ago when everybody's rent was raised and they believe that they just went out of business.

***

Two days later there was a call for Detective Simpson from the manager of Gladwyne Bank and Trust.

"Detective Simpson, this is Edward Morrissey. You asked me to call you if there was something that I thought would help you. It seems like my assistant was there the same day that William Spaulding opened Mrs. Moore's safe deposit box and the following day a customer of ours, Mr. Robert Snyder who manages Mrs. Moore's property, entered the safe to get access to his own safe deposit box. Honestly, I don't know what's going on but I just wanted to pass that information to you. Had I known that when you were here, I would've certainly informed you."

"Mr. Morrissey, thank you very much. That is very helpful. Once again if something else comes up please call me."

"Theo. I think we might have the break that we were looking for. Why in the world would Robert Snyder go to Gladwyne Bank and Trust to the safe deposit box in his name the day after William Spaulding was there?"

"Get Snyder's ass in here. That SOB has been playing with us. It's over. I want him in here with both of us," Harrison demanded.

Chapter 26

Simpson placed to call to Robert Snyder only to get his answering machine. He left the following message:

"Mr. Snyder. It is urgent that you come to this office immediately. You have 24 hours to get here."

Robert felt like a freshman after completing a walk-through at Temple Law School for post-graduate students. After finishing he drove to Amanda's apartment getting there before she did. He used the key that she had given him, laid his books on the countertop in the kitchen and made himself a cup of coffee. When the brew was ready he sat on one of the stools at the counter and flipped through some of his new law books. Moments later he reached for the phone and called his answering machine. Hearing the very emphatic message, he called Detective Simpson immediately.

"I received your call, detective, and you sound very upset. What can I do for you?"

"Mr. Snyder, I need you in my office immediately, with no excuses. I'm going to wait for you. Can I expect you shortly?"

"Yes, Detective. I'll leave now."

Robert left a note on the counter for Amanda simply stating: Detective wants me at the department immediately and I will call you on the way back. Love.

He rushed as quickly as possible navigating traffic jams but it still took him nearly an hour. He went to the police department headquarters then to the detective division where he found Simpson and Harrison both waiting for him. He had no idea what to expect.

"Mr. Snyder, where is the pistol?" Simpson, hands on hips, appeared very aggravated. Harrison also stood.

"Detectives, I told you. I sold it to a pawnshop several years ago. I have no idea what they did with it."

"Mr. Snyder, we know you went to your safe deposit box within 48 after Mrs. Moore was murdered. What caused you to go there?" Harrison demanded.

It was the first time that Robert Snyder had nothing to say. He looked at both of the detectives shrugged his shoulders. "What do you want me to tell you?"

"The truth goddamnit! Just the fucking truth!" a pissed off Harrison responded.

"Am I under arrest?"

Simpson spoke. "Not yet. You will be if we don't get answers."

"I'm sorry but I can't tell you."

"We want you to open up the safe deposit box," Harrison said. "If not, tomorrow we will get a court order to have it drilled open. I have already authorized the safe deposit box to be sealed."

"Detectives, I really want to cooperate but if I'm not being arrested I'm leaving. I'm going to get in touch with an attorney because I don't like the way this is going."

Robert waited for a response and hearing none he slowly turned around and headed back to his car. He had no idea what to do first, thinking he should call Bill Spaulding then figuring he had better discuss it with Amanda.

His mind was spinning. He never thought that anyone would associate his trip to the bank with the murder of Mrs. Moore.

How do I explain it to Amanda? Will she think that I killed Mrs. Moore? He had a nervous stomach on the trip back to Amanda's apartment. *I have to tell her something.*

***

By the time Robert returned to Amanda's apartment, she already had dinner on the table. Robert looked upset and he came over simply to hug her.

"Robert, what happened? You look like you so a ghost."

"I don't know where to start. I'm shook up and totally confused. The detectives wanted me to open up my safe deposit box and threatened that if I did not they would get a court order."

"What's going on?"

"They traced the records of my purchase of the 22-caliber pistol from years ago at Ruttenberg's. It confirmed everything that I told them, except when I told him that I sold it to a pawnshop. I lied. I did not sell it. I kept it all these years."

"You kept it?" an astonished Amanda asked. "But you told me that you sold it to a pawnshop. Why would you lie? And lie to me?"

"I used to keep it under my pillow for the months that I shared an apartment with those creepy guys. And when I moved I still continued doing it as a habit. When I went to work for Mrs. Moore and became comfortable in my surroundings, I stopped that habit and put it on the top of my clothes closet shelf. It remained there. I never touched it. Then after the detectives told me that Mrs. Moore was killed with a 22-caliber pistol I got worried whether my pistol was still there."

He took some deep breaths.

"I went to the closet and it wasn't in the corner where I placed it, but in the middle, which got me scared. Could someone have taken my pistol and killed the woman that I cared for and blamed me? So I took it and put it in the safe deposit box that I had. I was praying that they found somebody that did it and that no one ever used my gun."

"Robert, you have to tell the detectives. Perhaps there are some fingerprints that will point them in a direction other than you, or hopefully, they find after a ballistics test that your gun was never used for her murder. If I didn't have a caseload I would go with you."

"What if it is the gun that killed her? I'll go to jail. I didn't do anything but care for her. I'm scared."

Amanda had a nervous stomach. *What if the man she loves and is going to marry is a killer?*

"Do you want me to call them for you?" Amanda asked.

"No, I'll call them now." Robert then dialed to call Detective Harrison or Simpson.

Simpson answered, "Can I help you?"

"Yes, Detective. This is Robert Snyder. I have some things to discuss with you and I am willing to open my safe deposit box for your inspection and to take my pistol."

A shocked Simpson was confused. *If Snyder was the killer why would he volunteer to have us remove his pistol? Did he own more than one and was this one not used in the murder so that we are thrown a curve?*

"Where do you want me to meet you, detective since I want to discuss my actions?"

"How about at the bank tomorrow morning at 9:30? After that, we can drive to my office."

"I will be there, Detective. See you then."

Amanda was relieved that he was going to open up the safe deposit box. She believed that was the right thing to do and if he had nothing to do with the murder it would certainly be obvious that it wasn't him. She reheated the meal that she had prepared for him but he had no appetite. It was not a cause for celebration for either of them. All that each of them thought about was handing over the pistol and hoping it did not match the bullet that killed Mrs. Moore.

***

Taking a cup of coffee for the ride to Gladwyne Bank and Trust and fighting heavier than usual city traffic Robert still arrived at the bank on time. Detective Simpson's automobile was parked outside with him at the wheel.

179

"Let's see what's in the bank first and then we can have that discussion," Simpson instructed.

After cordial greetings to the assistant manager, the safe deposit vault was opened and Robert signed in handing the attendant his key. Box 304 was in Robert Snyder's name and its contents revealed to Detective Simpson.

Right in front of him was the 22-caliber semi-automatic pistol that Robert had purchased from Ruttenberg's in addition to his birth certificate, a baptismal certificate, his expired passport, and one expired driver's license. Simpson picked up the pistol by its finger guard using a pen and placed it in a plastic bag. The detective and Robert both thanked the attendant and assistant manager then departed.

"Mr. Snyder, would you mind following me to headquarters and then we can have whatever discussion you would like?"

"No problem," Robert Snyder replied, although he felt nervous.

Robert followed Simpson to his office. Harrison came over and signed the 22-caliber pistol into the evidence room. Robert apologized to both the detectives for not being truthful about the pistol when he said that he sold it to a pawnshop. He explained that he was scared and would not have taken the gun to put it in the safe deposit box had the police officers at the house not mentioned that it was a 22-caliber bullet. He went on to tell them about why he purchased the pistol years ago and how he used to keep it under his pillow until he actually got comfortable at Hampton Court. There was no doubt in his mind exactly where he placed the pistol on the right-hand side of the shelf in his closet where it remained for over a year. All he could think of was that he knew that he didn't kill Mrs. Moore but he was one of just a few people that had a key to the house and he lived on the property. He felt anyone from the outside looking at the situation would believe he is the number one suspect. He told the detectives that Stasha came knocking on his door screaming hysterically and when he opened the door she came in to tell him. He then ran to the house immediately, leaving Stasha behind.

After the police had done their investigation, he went back into his apartment. He looked for his 22-caliber pistol and saw it had been moved to the center of the shelf. Then he got really scared and figured that maybe the housekeeper had taken his pistol and used it to kill Mrs. Moore, though he seriously doubted it.

"Detectives, I didn't know what to do. I panicked. The next day I put the pistol in my safe deposit box. I apologize and pray that my pistol did not kill Mrs. Moore."

"We will know as soon as possible, Mr. Snyder. We don't do ballistics here. The pistol will have to be sent to the lab in Norristown. They have the latest technology there," Detective Harrison informed Robert.

"How soon can that be?"

"It's not like in books or television. This could take from a couple of weeks to a month or so, depending on the priority."

"I hope it's quick. I can't take much more of this," Robert said and left.

"Theo. Do you believe this guy?"

"I don't know who to believe. But I would check that housekeeper again. We've got nothing to lose while ballistics does their thing."

"I'll put this through for a priority if it helps."

Simpson once again opened the file, this time looking for Stasha or her boyfriend Aleksander's phone number. He waited till 6 p.m., believing that she would be home by then. and called her. She was home and the detective asked her for Aleksander's last name which she provided. Luschak. Aleksander Luschak. He has been living with her for seven years. She did not have a work telephone number for him. After hanging up the phone he ran a check to see what if anything came up and was shocked to find out that less than four years ago he was released from prison after serving five years for armed robbery. He certainly wasn't living with Stasha for seven years although it may have seemed like that.

181

Could she have provided Aleksander with a key to Hampton Court or innocently put it in her pocketbook and he stole it?

At 8 o'clock that evening he called back and Aleksandra was there. Simpson explained that he needed to talk with him and arranged to meet him at noon at a Wawa store at 22nd and Edgemont Avenue in Chester, Pennsylvania.

***

As Simpson pulled his car into the parking lot, he pretty much was able to discern who Aleksander was. Standing alongside the two glass entrance doors was an overweight, cigarette-smoking, and tattooed man fitting the description given by Robert Snyder.

He asked, "Are you Aleksander?" To which the man simply nodded his head up and down in confirmation as and exhaled a cigarette smoke ring.

"What is it you want from me?" he asked in a very deep and heavy Polish voice.

"I'm one of the detectives investigating the homicide at Hampton Court last December. I've been told that you were there weekly. Is there a place that we can sit down here?"

"No seating. Your car," he answered.

Simpson walked over to his Ford sedan and opened up the front passenger door letting Aleksander in and then sat in the front driver's seat.

"To set the record straight, I know you served five years from robbery so let's eliminate any bullshit. You went to the property where Stasha worked once a week .Mrs. Moore was killed which you know. Where were you that day that she was murdered?"

"Do I need lawyer?"

"Only if I arrest you. As I asked, where were you that day and the day before?"

"Mister detective. I work hard at auto body shop on Upland Avenue every day and some nights. Some days Stasha car breaks down and I have to take her to work. Some days she give her car to a friend to go to New Jersey to see her sick mother and I drive Stasha to work and then go to my job. Here is the card where I work. Call my boss. He got card when I sign in and when I leave. You want more, I call lawyer." Alek opened up the door and left.

***

When Simpson returned to the office, as usual, he updated Harrison.

"Harold, you can check everybody and I want you to; however, my gut says that this Robert Snyder did it and had the most to gain. He's sharp and don't forget that he is an actor. When the ballistics report comes back we're going to be sending out a warrant for his arrest. You mark my word. That doesn't mean that you slack off anything. Keep digging deeper. We were both wrong with that Billy Thompson. I don't wanna see that happen again. It's your future and my retirement. I don't want anything to interfere with it so roll up your sleeves and do the best that you can do." Harrison instructed Simpson and added,

"Take a good look at the timecards to see that nobody signed him in or out, which a lot of guys do for friends at work."

Chapter 27

Except for being a suspect in a murder case, Robert felt like a kid again when he started back to class at Temple University School of Law. This time his attitude was totally different. Instead of just studying to obtain good grades he wanted to study to learn and to excel. He realized from his experiences prior to working for Mrs. Moore, during his employ there and the subsequent ongoing investigations that he wanted to be a great attorney. Possibly a criminal attorney.

Every day after classes he wandered over to Mitten Hall where students congregated mostly to study but some to socialize. His sole intent was to study and study hard. After a few hours there he went to Amanda's apartment where he was spending more and more time.

By this time Amanda knew everything that Robert had told her about the ongoing investigation but she never told Robert that she still chatted with Detective Harrison and on occasion Detective Simpson to be in the loop. She was positive that Robert was innocent but still, until they found out the results of the ballistic report, she couldn't feel a true hundred percent positive. Since she was an assistant district attorney she used that to reach someone in ballistics at Montgomery County. She expressed her interest in knowing the results as soon as possible. They told her they would do the best that they could with no guarantees as to time.

Robert entered her apartment with a handful of books which he placed on the cocktail table to the left of the sofa. He saw Amanda coming out of the bedroom looking her gorgeous self as he walked towards her.

"You look exhausted, Robert. Too much studying?"

"This time I can never do too much studying. I want you to be proud of me and I want to be proud of myself. Every time I see you, you look more and more gorgeous. I'm a lucky guy to have you by my side and I appreciate you being supportive of me. I do not intend to disappoint you."

Every time Robert spoke Amanda would be upset with herself for ever doubting him. Tonight she didn't do any cooking, nor did he. On the way home from work she stopped at Foo Wok her favorite Chinese restaurant and brought home cartons filled with hot food. Robert enjoyed sitting at the counter instead of the formal dining room table. As he started to eat his dinner he leafed through some pages of one of his law books.

"I see you're really serious, Bobby, or should I now refer to you as Robert?"

"I just had something on my mind and I wanted to see if I understood it properly." He closed the book and reached over to kiss her.

"Mandy, I love you. More than you could ever imagine."

Thirty minutes later they were both finished eating and together they cleaned up the counter and kitchen. In the microwave was some hot saké, which she brought over to the sofa and placed the container on a bamboo trivet on the cocktail table. Robert poured the hot saké into two small cups.

"Did you study enough to relax?" Amanda asked Robert.

"Never too much but more than enough for my class assignment."

Amanda opened up a small sterling silver embossed jewelry box resting on the cocktail table. Inside were several rolled joints. She took a fireplace matchstick, smiling while looking at Robert, and lit it. After taking two long drags, she invited Robert to partake. Robert was sitting there and idolizing Amanda then just smiled as he reached over to accept her offering.

He went to put something on the CD and found Barry White's "Can't Get enough" and Rex Smith's "Take my Breath Away."

Amanda cuddled up in Robert's arms as Barry White's recording was playing. They were in another world of just the two of them closing out everything else from their minds.

A night of love and caring continued seemingly forever.

***

The smell of fresh coffee awakened Robert. Amanda wanted to please him even though her presence was all that he needed and wanted.

Once the coffee took effect Robert was back to thinking about the upcoming ballistics report and what would that do to his relationship with Amanda.

Amanda, standing on the other side of the counter wearing his undershirt and no panties, wasn't thinking about the ballistics report. She had other things on her mind.

As sensuous as she looked, Robert opened up one of his law books and started to read.

"Mandy, you want me to do great don't you? I know you do. Just give me a half-hour to absorb this and then we will absorb each other."

Without saying a word she walked behind Robert and took his right hand off the book that he was reading and put it between her thighs.

"I may not be able to wait for you."

Robert placed his bookmarker in the spot that he was reading, closed the book, and made love to her in the kitchen. He never got back to his book that day.

Chapter 28

Simpson took his notebook and headed for Marvel Auto Body Collision on Upland Avenue to meet with Anthony Cordone, the owner. Anthony was very friendly and explained that he knew Alek's background and that he was a good worker. He then went into his secretary's office to open up the filing cabinet where prior timecards were stored. Simpson gave him the date of the homicide and within moments he found the timecard. It appeared as though Alek had worked the second shift that day coming in at 2 p.m. then signing out for a thirty-minute lunch break at 6 p.m. and then finally signing out at 9:54 p.m.

Simpson asked the secretary to make a photocopy of the card, plus one for the day before and the day after just so they could check the patterns. He thanked everyone for their help and headed back to headquarters.

Once again he updated Detective Harrison and showed him the cards. Harrison picked up the fact that the following day the card shows that Alek checked in at work at 8 a.m.

"He must be an extremely busy person if he left work at 9:54 p.m., drove from Chester to Gladwyne, rampaged the house and killed Mrs. Moore, then somehow got back home, supposedly slept and was back at work by 8 a.m.," Harrison commented.

"I don't think anyone could get there in much less than one hour from the body shop and that's if there's no traffic," Simpson responded.

"That still comes easily within what the medical examiner thought was the timeline of death."

"I'm going to call that smart ass back," Simpson said. "I want to check what kind of car he drives and then tell him someone spotted it in the area. Let's see how he reacts."

Before doing that Simpson placed a call back to Anthony Cordone to ask him what kind of car Alek drives. The secretary paged Anthony, who was in the back of the shop where he picked up the phone. There was all kind of the hammering and banging typical of a body shop.

"Mr. Cordone. I'm sorry to bother you but I'm just checking on the type of automobile that Alek drives."

"Back then he had an Oldsmobile 88 coupe but wrecked it sometime last December. It's still sitting in the back. He was waiting for a front A-frame section but I told him he might as well just junk the car rather than spending time and money to put it together."

"May I ask how he got to work then and now if his car was wrecked?" inquired Simpson.

"Oh, that's easy, Detective. I lent him our loaner car with our sign painted on the doors and the trunk. He just keeps up the gas and service. I don't charge him to use it because he is a good worker. Plus people see my advertisement wherever he goes thinking that he's a customer. Take a look on the back of my business card. It shows a picture of the car. Underneath it says, 'Always a free loaner for a good customer.' "

A dejected Simpson again thanked the shop owner and reported to Harrison that he can't imagine anyone driving a painted-up automobile with signs all over it trying to sneak into a place without being noticed. Yet Harrison directed Simpson to speak with Aleksander because he still could have used someone else's automobile. Then he told him to confirm his whereabouts that night.

Simpson felt it was another worthless trip but he arranged to meet Aleksander in two days since he was working two day shifts in a row.

Chapter 29

More than two weeks went by without having any contact with either Detective Simpson or Harrison. The thought of the pistol being the one that killed Mrs. Moore hung like the proverbial albatross around Robert's neck. But this albatross also was hanging around Amanda's neck. It would be impossible for her to have absolutely no doubts about Robert, yet she did everything to push any negative thoughts out of her mind. Anytime she wasn't busy at work at the district attorney's office her thoughts focused on Robert. This is the young man that she loves and wants to marry but until Mrs. Moore's murderer is discovered, she's uncertain. One night with Robert lying by her side in a sound sleep she prayed that this would come to a good end.

     Robert called her office at lunchtime knowing that she would be there. He used a payphone at Mitten Hall since he did not have another class for 45 more minutes. While he was reading some case law, out of the clear blue some thoughts came into his mind. He told Amanda that he remembered apologizing to his friend and confidant Bill Spaulding for not calling him until after the police and medical examiner left the premises instead of calling him as soon as he found out that Mrs. Moore was murdered.

"This is terrible," Bill Spaulding had said to him. "Who in the world would do such a thing? What is there that's worth anything? Her paintings? Nobody would do such a thing to steal the paintings; they're too traceable."

How did Bill Spaulding even know what was stolen and how did he know that no one ever stole the paintings? Robert knew that he never told him. And Bill Spaulding had a key to the house. Robert wasn't certain if he ever told the detectives. And years ago it was Bill Spaulding that told him to go to Ruttenberg's and purchase a Colt Jr. 22-caliber pistol since it was small enough to keep in his pocket or under his pillow.

"Amanda. Am I going crazy? None of this makes any sense to me" Robert sounded confused and upset.

"Bobby, calm down. There's no way that Spaulding did anything like that. Why in the world would he do it?"

"I have some things to tell you when you get home. I have one last class that's over at 3:30, so I'll be there at four and wait for you."

"Bobby, I will be there at 4 o'clock. Just relax."

Robert could barely keep his mind on his studies. He dreaded the time that he would have to tell Amanda about the proposal that Bill Spaulding had made to him.

***

Both Robert and Amanda reached the portico at 1700 Rittenhouse at the same time. He didn't reach out to hug and kiss her but just to hold her hand which he did very tightly. Not a word was spoken until they both entered Amanda's apartment.

Robert asked her to sit down on the sofa and he sat next to her holding her hand.

"When we first met here at your apartment I was overwhelmed with how successful you were and what a failure was. I told you that I had taken the job basically to take care of everything to do with Mrs. Moore and the estate of Hampton Court. It was through Bill Spaulding, who was my agent and a friend since our days at Temple. He became a lawyer and eventually a partner with this prestigious firm but still never gave up being an agent for actors. He had advanced me money for years and I had nothing but small parts in plays. Then one day he called me to tell me that he's got a good job for me that will pay well. I remember that day. I thought I was going to get an acting job in a major production but those were my dreams and he brought me down to reality. He told me that his client needed someone to oversee her property and to take her to medical appointments, which included physical therapy and trips to Pennsylvania Hospital. He told me the job would pay $750 a week plus the use of an automobile and a lovely carriage house apartment on the estate. He also told me that she was dying from some type of tumor on her brain and did not know how long she would live but he wanted me to be there to comfort her and to help her with whatever her needs were. He then told me that if I do a good job he is sure that I will be placed in her will. That if I was placed in her will and she subsequently passed on, he wanted one third whatever I may receive.

I never took the job to get included in her will. That meant nothing to me. I was disappointed that I wasn't having an opportunity to be in the theater but at the same time, I wasn't able to pay my own bills. He was such a good friend to me for so many years and he was going to recommend me for the position. I found it impossible to turn down. He told me that when he initially represented me many years before that I signed a contract with him which I remember was a typical representation contract that he would get a percentage of my future earnings. There were no future earnings and he had advanced me a lot of money to pay many of my bills. Even with odd jobs tending bar and waiting tables, each month I found myself a little bit more in debt. He wrote up a new contract and it stated that he would get one third. He then told me that he wanted the automobiles since he loves collecting cars and that Mrs. Moore's deceased husband had collected some very desirable automobiles. I didn't care about the cars, nor did I care about being in the will. He handed me $500 in cash and told me to get a new suit and a haircut for an interview. He gave me the date that the advertisement was going to be in the Philadelphia newspaper and told me to apply for the job just like everybody else and that if it's a close call he will recommend me.

"As it turned out she was such a wonderful woman to be with that I felt great doing the work. I loved it there. It was the first time in many years that I felt comfortable sleeping at night. After Mrs. Moore was murdered I had no thoughts about anything in the will. No one had mentioned a thing to me until after the funeral. Bill called me to tell me that I'm the sole beneficiary of everything that she owned. I literally didn't pay attention to anything he said. I was so upset that she was dead. We had just come back from dinner after having a great time.

"Then Bill told me that the real estate market was terrible and mortgage rates were astronomical that nobody was purchasing homes. He suggested some brokers because there was no way that I wanted to live in that home. I could not even afford the taxes. I had no income after she passed away. Then he told me that the contract states that I must pay him one-third of my worth after 30 days. He said he knew some brokers that deal with investment properties and there's someone that will buy the place who is willing to wait for the market to change if it ever did. They had an offer that was, according to him, very low but he suggested that I take it since he needed the one third immediately because he made a bad investment. He handled everything. I went to settlement. The sale of the home was $750,000. Out of the settlement, Bill took $250,000 plus $50,000 extra, which still left me a lot of money. More money than I've ever seen in my life. He also explained to me that the state inheritance tax had to be paid immediately, which was 15% of the $900,000 since the old cars were worth $150,000 according to Bill. I still thought I had a lot of money. Then Bill wanted the titles signed over to him, which I had agreed to. Later the accountant figured out that after I paid the money due on April 15 to the IRS that I'd wind up with about $75,000. I'm confused. I trusted him and I still do but something doesn't seem right."

***

The following morning as soon as she arrived at work, Amanda placed a phone call to Detective Harrison's office inquiring about the ballistics report. He was out so she left a message to please contact her and bring her up-to-date with anything else of significance about the case. She then called the district attorney's office in Montgomery County asking if they would, as a courtesy, get her the results from the forensic lab including reports and photographs of the bullet that killed Mrs. Moore and the photographs and results of the bullet from the 22-caliber Colt pistol that they were testing. She gave the assistant DA her mailing address at City Hall and asked him to mark the envelope 'Personal.'

The next thing she did was to contact two real estate agents that specialize in upscale properties in the Gladwyne area. She asked one agent about Hampton Court and if he knew the value of that property. He had no information to help her but informed her that the real estate market has been exceptionally soft over the last couple years. She then placed a call to another real estate agent who knew of the property and informed her that it will be listed very shortly. He said currently it is a 'pocket listing,' explaining that the brokerage firm has not yet placed it on the exchange. To her surprise, the price was a firm $2.5 million, including furnishings and decorations. Amanda asked who the owner was and the agent was not able to provide her the name, only that it was purchased by a corporation.

Later that same day she had an idea and contacted a friend of hers who works for a real estate title company and gave him the address of Hampton Court. He informed her that the information that she was seeking would take just a few days.

***

Robert was attending law school classes and that week was his first quiz. He was thrilled when his professor remarked to the entire class that he had scored the highest.

He felt like the old man since all the other students were nearly ten years his junior.

***

Nearly a week later, Amanda received a manila folder from the District Attorney's Office of Montgomery County addressed to her personally. She opened it and found two reports. She skimmed through them until she found what she was looking for. The Colt Jr. 22-caliber pistol serial number 59711CC that was recovered from Robert Snyder's safe deposit box definitely was not the pistol that fired the 22-caliber bullet that killed Mrs. Jacqueline Phyliss Moore.

An ecstatic Amanda screamed out loud, "Thank God!" There was no one in her office; however, two people came running in from the adjacent office wondering if she was OK.

She assured both of them that everything was wonderful.

She knew that she could not contact Robert since he was at school but would have great news when he came to her apartment at dinner time. Once the adrenaline stopped pumping, she wondered why Detective Harrison or Detective Simpson never called her. They certainly would've been the first to be informed of the results before she received them in the mail. Then she thought, *perhaps they're just too lazy.*

Amanda checked out two hours early to have a surprise for Robert. She stopped at a flower shop and purchased yellow daffodils. She then went to a boutique women's store and purchased a sexy Teddy. She then went to a sleazy adult video store on Race Street and purchased some sex tapes. Stopping at the local butcher shop she picked up two large well-aged sirloin strip steaks. Her last stop was to a local smoke shop where she purchased a bong. The last time she used one was years ago, at a party at one of the frat houses on campus at Temple.

At home, everything was arranged for a night to remember.

She placed the two steaks after rubbing them with olive oil and sprinkling them lightly with liquid Maggie in the oven to preheat. On the top of the gas range, she had a black cast-

195

iron frying pan warming and waiting to accept the steaks once they reached the proper temperature. Two glasses of Burgess Cabernet Sauvignon 1974 vintage were one-third filled waiting to be consumed by the two lovers. On the record player was Cool and the Gang's top recording, "Celebration." In the center of the cocktail table was the Bong ready to be used.

Amanda had notified the doorman to call her as soon as Robert pulled up. Her phone rang.

"He just arrived."

She turned on the music having the volume very loud. She had inflated balloons that were tied together with ribbons. Robert entered and was stunned.

"Is today July 4?" he asked rhetorically.

"It's time to celebrate, Robert. You have been completely and irrevocably exonerated. The test results proved that your pistol was not involved at all in Mrs. Moore's death."

Totally relieved, Robert cast his legal books aside, grabbed Amanda by the waist, and started dancing in a circle as if they were at a gypsy wedding.

He rattled off question after question from the excitement. "How do you know? Who got the ballistics test? Did they find the real killer?"

Amanda calmed him down and explained receiving the envelope with the test results but no, they haven't found a killer. She also was a little bit perturbed that neither of the detectives ever informed her and obviously they did not inform Robert of the ballistics report.

Robert, seeing the balloons and hearing "Celebration" blasting, gave her the most passionate kiss in either of their lives. He knew more than ever how much he loved her and that she felt the exact same way. Amanda handed Robert the glass of Cabernet Sauvignon then reached into the oven to take the steaks and put them into the waiting black skillet. She looked at Robert and removed a lightweight outer jacket to reveal her voluptuous body ever so lightly covered by the delicate Teddy.

"Mandy. Forget the steaks. I want to make you my meal."

"Just be patient, Robert. We're going to be celebrating all night long."

Walking around wearing barely anything, Amanda had the flames on the gas range set to high underneath the skillet waiting for the heat to rise. Robert just stood there watching her as his flames pulsated throughout his body. Then she placed the steaks into the pan which sizzled. Mandy had made her own sauce béarnaise and a pan of seared thinly-sliced potatoes in another skillet. She was trying to duplicate the meals that Robert talked so much about when he took Mrs. Moore to dinner at Blue Bell Inn.

She made a small slice into one of the sirloin strips; it was rare inside and burnt on the outside. Just like they both wanted it.

Dinner was served on the dining room table. Even though there was room to seat eight to ten people, the two of them sat opposite each other enjoying the meal and contemplating a wonderful evening of romance.

Robert enjoyed the meal more than anything he had ever eaten before because this was something extra special. Amanda put her heart and soul into the meal so that Robert could enjoy it. After dinner, they curled up on the rug in front of the fireplace and Amanda and Robert inhaled the bong. Before long they were both giddy and totally immersed in each other.

***

The following morning it was back to work for Amanda and off to law school for Robert. When Amanda arrived at her office there was a message for her to call Detective Harrison.

Without hesitation, she called Harrison, who promptly answered the phone. He informed her that he just received the forensic results from ballistics and that he concurred that Robert was definitely not complicit in the murder of Mrs. Moore. Amanda felt that the detective actually sounded disappointed that it wasn't Robert.

"Detective Harrison. What other leads are you working on and is there anything that I can do with the help of our office here in Philadelphia?"

Harrison replied that he really thought that Robert did it and he's going to have to go over everything yet again with a fine-tooth comb. He updated her with information about Stasha's boyfriend, Alek, and said that Simpson was heading there again to fill in some blanks. He told her honestly that he's at a dead end.

She asked what they found out, if anything, about the whereabouts of William Spaulding that evening. He told her they confirmed that he was home the evening of the homicide. She didn't mention anything about the relationship that Bill Spaulding had formed with Robert. She would confirm everything herself because she felt that the detectives were incompetent. Amanda never mentioned that she already knew the results of the ballistics test that was sent to her from the DAs office in Montgomery County.

***

"This is Amanda Dillington calling from the district attorney's office in Philadelphia to speak with William Spaulding Esquire."

Seconds later. "This is William Spaulding, may I help you?"

"Mr. Spaulding. I have been told that you are also an artistic agent and that you represented one Robert Snyder for many years. Am I correct?"

"Not just represented him but I've considered him a dear friend for many years. Is there something that I can do for you, Ms. Dillington?"

"Yes, there is. In speaking with Robert he informed me that many years back he signed a representation contract with you and a couple years ago it was updated. I would like a copy of both of those contracts if that is possible."

"I'll have to see. He was one of the last few that I represented. But somewhere around here, I'm sure I'll find it. Is there a problem? Is Robert all right?"

"From my last conversation with him, he was excellent and enjoying his new classes at Temple. He speaks so highly of you. I'm a personal friend from back at Temple and I am certain that I must have met you a decade ago."

"Is there a problem?"

"I certainly hope not. Just trying to help him out."

Amanda gave Bill Spaulding her mailing address and fax number asked him to please send her a copy of both representation contracts. He assured her that he would make a sincere effort to find them as quickly as he could.

Amanda had put everything on hold regarding Robert since her department was working with the FBI on an investigation involving three corrupt politicians. She had to keep everything pretty close to her vest, as she was not certain who in her department might be feeding information to the politicians involved. It was a difficult situation for her since she would have loved to confide with others in her office but was uncertain who to trust. Many times she had meetings out of the office with FBI agents and simply gave excuses to be off premises.

Chapter 30

Simpson met with Aleksander and questioned him as to his whereabouts the evening that he worked till 9:54 p.m. He tried to think and told the detective that he really wasn't sure.

"It was a vile ago. How I remember that long ago? Do you?" a very sarcastic Alek replied. "I probably go home. Maybe I stopped at bar and take two beers ?"

"Look, Alek. If you don't want to sit in jail until you remember, you better give me an answer now. If not I'm taking you in. I had enough of your sarcastic shit!"

Simpson was out of character but getting aggravated.

"I was with a hooker. I'll give you her name. It's on the back of dis card." In pencil on the back of the business card from the body shop that was the name Irene and a phone number. "$20 and all night. Good body. Good mechanic. You call her. She call me big boy."

Simpson asked how long he was with her. Alek said two hours maybe all night and he gave the detective her address. Simpson drove to a private home and knocked on the door and

Irene opened it just a little bit, keeping the safety chain lock in place. He could see her wearing a housecoat and it was obvious she had nothing on underneath. He thought he'd find some old washed-up hooker but instead found a girl in her mid-20s that was not half bad looking and built very well from what he could see. Simpson explained that he is a detective I needed some information from her. He assured her that he has no interest in whatever she does. He explained that Alek gave him her name and address. After hesitating just a moment she closed the door and removed the safety chain.

It turned out that Alek visits her weekly and she had dates circled on the calendar. There it was. The current calendar had last December and the night of Mrs. Moore's murder. He had been there all night.

Irene asked him did he want to stay for a while. He thought about it then just shook his head no but thanked her.

Once again frustrated, he headed back to headquarters.

***

While Amanda was working with the FBI on a Tuesday afternoon she started to remember a case going back about seven or eight years before where a woman was murdered in her home in the Oak Lane section of Philadelphia off of Godfrey Avenue. The case was never solved. Something that Robert had said sounded familiar. The homicide victim's husband had a car collection. That simple flash filled her mind and then she was back discussing their ongoing investigation involving the politicians.

The title search came back and Amanda's friend relayed the information. The ownership was WASP Principal Partners Inc. a private corporation whose actual owners are unknown. She then asked her friend to find out who filed the papers for the private corporation and to let her know.

That evening back at her apartment she brought Robert up to date. He was shocked that the house is selling for two and a half million dollars, especially when his friend Bill told him to accept the $750,000 offer. Robert still defended Bill Spaulding by telling Amanda that Bill had said the house is selling cheaply but since the agreement said 30 days, Robert was forced to accept the deal.

"I don't get a good vibe about your friend Spaulding. I think he's hiding something. When I asked him about getting a copy of your contract he made it appear that it's going to be somewhat difficult to find. I'm digging deeper."

***

A few days passed and surprisingly in Amanda's mail was a copy of the contract showing that Robert Snyder is represented by William Spaulding. For sums advanced and efforts extended to promote Robert Snyder, William Spaulding is entitled to receive one-third of any newly acquired income and or wealth within 30 days of receipt of such fund(s).

"So he did have an interest in the demise of Mrs. Moore," Amanda said out loud even though no one was there. "But that still doesn't mean that he had any involvement in her murder."

"Mr. Spaulding's office. May I help you?" Darlene, the secretary, answered the phone.

"Good morning. This is Amanda Dillington calling for Mr. Spaulding. I wanted to thank him for being so prompt and sending me the representation contract. May I speak with him?"

"I'm sorry but Mr. Spaulding took off today and is working on his old car again."

"Is he at his house in Bala Cynwyd?" Amanda inquired. "I'll see if I can take a ride over to thank him personally. If not when you hear from him ask him to please call me."

Amanda left her office, taking the Schuylkill Expressway to Bala-Cynwyd. She knew the address on Monument Road since Robert had told her. It was easy to find the very beautiful Tudor-styled home. As she pulled into the driveway, to her left was the three-car garage. One of the garage doors was open and she saw that someone was working beneath an old Mercedes.

From beneath the car, someone asked, "Who is it?"

"Mr. Spaulding. I wanted to come personally to thank you for sending me your representation contract of Robert."

Bill, lying on his back, slid out from beneath the car looking very surprised. He reached for the Go-Jo hand cleaner in the container on the wall quickly wiping his hands so he could shake hers.

"There was no need to come here. I said I would do it. It was nothing at all."

"Well, I really wanted to ask you something out of the office. Between us, how did you ever get Mrs. Moore to make Robert Snyder her sole beneficiary of everything that she owned?"

"I didn't. She requested it. She had a couple of relatives that never ever called her during her many years. I believe one or two nephews and nieces. She told me how much she cared about Robert and her health was getting better which she credited Robert for. I suggested just give him a token amount but she insisted. I even can let you hear the tape recording of our meeting. I recorded it strictly because I wanted to have the notes to prepare an update for her will." He continued, "If you give me a few minutes I'll have it for you. I brought the entire file home. It's in my office in my house. Do you want to come in?"

"If you don't mind, I'll wait out here. You have a very pretty car and I love your property."

Bill went into the house and Amanda just walked around the property keeping herself visible from the front door. She didn't want Bill to think that she was sneaking around. Moments later Bill came out with the tape recorder and played it for her. She was quite surprised. He told the truth. On the recording, he was suggesting that Mrs. Moore put aside a minimum amount for Robert but she insisted on giving him everything.

Amanda pulled out the settlement sheet from the sale of Hampton Court.

"By the way, Mr. Spaulding. It looks like you handled the settlement for Robert Snyder. Who was the purchaser?"

"It's on there. Some investment group."

Gene Epstein

"So it looks like you received over $300,000 from the sale of the home plus Robert handed you $150,000 worth of automobiles which was your appraised value. Quite a hefty sum wouldn't you say?"

"Ms. Dillington, I would suggest that you leave. I gave you all the information and I did not lie about anything. This discussion is over. From now on if you wish to speak to me do it at my office and not my home. You are not welcome here."

"Mr. Spaulding, thank you for your time. Next time will be at your office. And there will be a next time."

Amanda knew that he was a smart attorney. He has shown that he had covered all his bases. Possibly unethical but not illegal. She wasn't done. It only made her more determined to find out the real truth.

The next morning she had an idea. WASP Principal Partners Inc. was incorporated in the State of Pennsylvania. Amanda called the Pennsylvania Bureau of Corporations to find out if they had the names of the principles of the corporation. After being switched from one person to another over the course of twenty minutes she did reach someone that was able to tell her that the corporation is a private corporation and that they could only supply the name the incorporator. It was William Aaron Spaulding, Esquire.

"Got him," she said to herself.

"Mr. Spaulding's office. May I help you?"

"Yes. I'm calling from the District Attorney's Office. This is Amanda Dillington, assistant district attorney. Please put William Spaulding on the line immediately," she insisted.

After a minute, the secretary got back on the phone. "Mr. Spaulding is too busy to speak with you now. Perhaps another time?"

"Tell him I am on my way over to his office."

Even though there was rain in the forecast, Amanda walked from her office in City Hall to his office just a few blocks away. She went to Calhoun, Spaulding, and Feingold and met Darlene in person.

204

"I am Amanda Dillington. Tell Mr. Spaulding I'm here."

Darlene buzzed his office and informed him of her presence. He was noticeably upset.

"Tell her I'm with a client and she'll have to wait."

Amanda sat patiently for nearly a half-hour. She realized he had to be pissed off that she's at his office. But she was more than patient, realizing that he must be getting upset not knowing what was on her mind. Then Darlene informed Amanda that she could go in.

"What is it that you want now ?" Spaulding sat back with his arms folded.

"Well, Mr. Spaulding you told me that the property was sold to an investment group. I checked the records at the State of Pennsylvania Bureau of Corporations and the buyer WASP Principle Partners Inc. was formed by you. You actually purchased the property that belonged to Robert Snyder but you never told him that you were the buyer. On the contrary, you told him it was an investment group."

"It was and is an investment group. So maybe I purchased the property cheaply. That's not against the law."

"It certainly is unethical not informing your client— whom you encouraged to sell the property—that you were the hidden buyer. I don't think that the Pennsylvania Supreme Court Disciplinary Board would feel you did right by your client," she said standing there with her hands on her hips.

"Counselor. Are you threatening me?" he asked.

"You will know, Mr. Spaulding when I am threatening you."

Amanda left the office. Since it was getting close to the end of the workday, she just walked home not worrying about the overcast skies. When she arrived she was surprised that Robert was already there.

"Short day?" she asked.

"The professor of my last class had an emergency and left early. So we all went home. What's happening with you?"

Amanda went on to tell him that she felt that his good friend, agent, and attorney scammed him out of several hundred thousand dollars, if not more. Robert was shocked.

He refused to believe it. Amanda laid out the facts and it finally sunk into his head that Bill used him simply to enrich himself.

"But he would not have killed her. That is totally impossible. He may have conned me because I was susceptible but he would never do anything like that."

"It seems as though he has an answer for everything that he did, even if something was shady. I think he is covering up more than I am exposing. I am not stopping. I'll get to the bottom of this."

Amanda suggested that they go to the Ritz theater since that month featured old Alec Guinness movies. That evening's film was *The Lady Killers*.

* * *

At the office the following morning Amanda started looking through old files from when she had first started in the District Attorney's office years before. She was very upset that William Spaulding was playing games with her thinking that he could outsmart her. Not finding anything that she was looking for, she asked a previous assistant D.A. who was now working in the governor's office in the State of Delaware. She called her old friend and associate Thomas Paul asking if he remembered a similar case where a widow, who was murdered in her home, had a previous husband who collected classic cars. All he could say was that something sounded familiar but nothing that he remembered. She wouldn't give up; going once again through the files trying to find a link.

She asked Sid Ginsberg, one of the detectives that she worked with, if he knew of any homicides in the East Oak Lane section involving an elderly woman that was unsolved.

"I do. I think it was on 11th St. One of the big old stately homes. It was about a half a mile from the Hot Shoppe restaurant where we used to go for our morning coffee. At that time I was working out of the 35th Police District at Broad St and Champlost Avenue."

"That's great. Any chance you have a name or an address or possibly both?" Amanda requested.

206

"I really don't, I'm sorry. If you give me a couple days...I remember what the house looked like on 11th St. so I can at least get you an address. Does that help?"

"Anything will help. Sid, I really appreciate the time and effort. I'll wait for your call."

Amanda felt there was a possibility that with an address she could track down more information.

***

Two days later Amanda received a phone call from Sid Ginsberg. The house was actually on 69th Ave. where it met 11th St. The Knoblock family resides there now and he asked them if they remembered who the seller was. They said it was some investment real estate company.

Amanda called Sid back immediately. "Sid. That's great. Would you happen to know if it was WASP real estate?"

"That's it. They kept mentioning letters, and yes, that is definitely it."

"Do me a favor. Just keep this to yourself. I'm just checking on something for a friend and it's nothing I want to be out there in public."

Now having the address, Amanda had to find out who was the owner prior to WASP. She called her friend at the title company once again. She needed a search back over the last decade. Searching the records at the courthouse would take a couple of days being that it is very tedious work. Since it was Friday she probably would not have an answer until the following Tuesday. She would never have delved into this to such an extent if it wasn't that she felt that William Spaulding used the person that she loved and played him for a fool.

***

At 2 o'clock Monday afternoon she received a call from the title company.

"Do you have a pencil, Amanda? Or I can fax this over to you."

She gave him the fax number for her office at City Hall and two minutes later, there it was. Herman and Gloria Goldman prior owners. Then to Armand Krouse and flipped to WASP Principal Partners Inc.

"Sidney, does the name Gloria Goldman sound familiar to you?" Amanda asked.

"Yes. Yes. You got it."

"Thanks for the confirmation, Sid."

Amanda ran through different scenarios in her mind. If this Gloria Goldman was shot with a 22-caliber pistol and Bill Spaulding's private corporation purchased her house, there certainly seems to be a pattern but it all could be coincidental. Now having the date that the home was sold and the date of the prior sale she needed to find out about the homicide.

She was keeping everything to herself not letting anyone know anything else other than what she had requested of them. At this point, she went into the homicide records for one year preceding the sale of the home to WASP Principal Partners Inc.

Once she was in the file room and found the year, she was surprised to find that the files were quite large. There were numerous homicides that year. More than many. Fanning through one file after the other, it wasn't long until she saw Gloria Goldman, 77 years old. Widow. No next of kin.

In the notes written by two detectives was that someone broke into the house attempting to steal rare antiques. It appeared as though Gloria Goldman must have surprised the thief, who shot her in the head, killing her immediately. A person living on the property was questioned since he was the caretaker and helped her manage her doctor's appointments, medications, and the estate. No weapon was found. There were color photographs and Spectro Eye graphs of the bullet that was removed from her head. Amanda photocopied every page of the file including the ballistics report and Spectro Eye graphs.

She thought about calling Detective Harrison to get the photographs of the bullet in the spectrograph but changed her mind. She did not want him to know what she was investigating because she had her own plan. She then contacted the same person at Montgomery County who had sent her the ballistics report to please send her copies of the actual bullet. Also, if they would release that bullet to her to be compared with another bullet by the FBI. In order to do it, she would have to send them a request and was informed how to do it. She then called the Philadelphia Fire Arms Identification Unit. They also agreed to release the bullet to her custody providing the proper form was filled out.

After knowing that she could obtain the actual bullets from both homicides, she asked the FBI agent to compare the two to see if both had the same markings, so identifying that one pistol had killed two people. She did not want a report in writing. Simply whether or not they matched.

Amanda was surprised that she enjoyed doing the work that the detectives should have done correctly more than she did being an assistant district attorney.

She filled out all the papers that were required and sent them to both agencies. The following week she received calls from both ballistic departments that the bullets should be picked up in person and signed for.

Having a heavy caseload and being close to being able to prosecute three politicians it was several days until she was found the time to break away.

In less than an hour's drive from her office, Amanda arrived at the Montgomery County Courthouse Ballistics Department. She presented proper identification and was given the bullet in a cloth bag strung tight at the top with an accompanying tag on it showing a case number, file number, and name of the victim, Mrs. Jacqueline Phyliss Moore.

Back at her office, which she considered her home away from home, she called down to the Ballistics Department and arranged to pick up the bullet that killed Gloria Goldman.

Each bullet was bagged differently. She presented it to the FBI agent the following morning who was sending it down to Virginia to be compared. He explained that this will take a few more days.

***

Back home she tried to relax with Robert without giving him all the details of what had transpired over the past two weeks. She didn't want to get his hopes up nor be disappointed. He certainly had gone through enough waiting for the report about the pistol that he owned to be cleared of murder charges.

Robert was pretty much totally immersed in his law studies and enjoying it, not as a prelude to a position but enjoying learning more and more about the legal system.

Amanda was close to winning the combined case of criminal charges for graft and associated charges against three well-known Philadelphia politicians. She worked with fervor alongside the FBI agents that were called in on the case.

Over a week later, the agent that she was working with handed her a manila folder that was clipped at the top and taped across with the words in bold print "Personal and Confidential."

She sat at a desk and with a letter opener carefully cut through the tape and there it was. The report from FBI Ballistics confirming that both bullets were fired from the same pistol. Only one other person knew that and she was going to call him before the day was out.

"William Spaulding's office. May I help you?" asked a very cordial Darlene.

"Yes, Darlene. This is assistant district attorney Dillington. Find William Spaulding immediately and I will accept no excuses," she demanded.

"What is it now?" he asked.

"William. I want you to be at my apartment this evening at 7 o'clock. I strongly suggest you give me no excuses. Plain and simple—be there."

"What's going on? Who do you think you are talking to like that? An assistant D.A. that will never go anywhere."

"Well Bill, it's like this. Before I institute multiple murder charges against you since we have a lock tight case, it's your choice. Be at my apartment promptly at 7 p.m. or tomorrow morning you will be handcuffed and taken to jail, that will probably lead to your execution."

She paused.

"Now do you want my address?"

There was a deafening silence.

"Yes, please give me the address."

Chapter 31

At precisely 7 o'clock that evening there was a knock on her apartment door. She opened it and William Spaulding Esquire was standing there. Amanda invited him in. She pointed to her sofa indicating that she wanted him to sit down. On the cocktail table in front of the sofa were two bottles of wine. One Chardonnay. One Cabernet Sauvignon.

"This may take a while, so if you don't mind, I'll call you Bill. Would you like a glass of wine? Your preference?"

"Do you have any Scotch? I'm not really a wine drinker."

"Absolutely." Amanda reached into the liquor cabinet and pulled out a bottle of Chivas Regal and poured him a glass on the rocks.

"Bill, we have a serious problem. I'm torn between two options and which one will be your choice."

"The first indication that something did not make sense to Robert was when he informed you that Mrs. Moore was murdered. Your reply was questioning why somebody would do that when there was nothing to steal and nobody took any paintings anyway. By the way, I want to tip my hat to you for tape recording Mrs. Moore's request that Robert be the sole heir to her estate. Very smart and your defense of Robert to the detectives was commendable. It certainly would deflect any concern that you were involved. You set Robert up from the beginning. You came through the gate and used your key to enter and shot her in the head while she was in bed. You then threw things all around the room as though there was an attempted burglary that went bad. Good job. No kidding. Several years before you encouraged Robert to purchase a Colt 22 Junior pistol, directing him to Ruttenberg's as you also did to Carmen Brancotta another theatrical student. Let's put all that aside. You pressured Robert to sell the house telling him that you needed the money because you had made a bad investment. You wrote an agreement stating that after any basically newfound wealth you would be entitled to one-third of that wealth within 30 days. You told Robert that there was a broker who had an offer for $750,000 from an investor to purchase Hampton Court, including all furnishings, and that he should take it since he had only 30 days to pay your fee. We both know the house was worth over $2 million at the time, not counting any of the furnishings or decorations. At settlement, you received a check for $250,000 plus approximately $50,000 in legal fees. This was after you told Robert that he would net nearly $500,000."

Bill interrupted, "Where are you going with this?"

"I told you, Bill, that when we're done I'm going to leave you the option. Now shut up and let me continue. At settlement you had Robert sign over the titles to the antique automobiles that you told him were sort of a bonus for everything that you did for him and that the cars were worth $150,000 when in reality the 1932 Duesenberg alone was worth a half a million dollars and the Mercedes Gullwing was worth nearly that, but let's not quibble. At that point, you had only defrauded Robert of somewhere between one and two million dollars. Several years before that you met a young man who was also an unsuccessful actor named Carmen Brancotta. You got him a job taking care of an elderly woman named Gloria Goldman in East Oak Lane whose husband also was deceased and had left several automobiles including a 1931 Chrysler LeBaron Dual Cowl four-door convertible, a 1937 Cord supercharged roadster and a 1953 Corvette convertible, one of the first ones built. Coincidently, you were the executor of her estate also, and she left everything to Carmen. That poor lady was shot in the head with a 22-caliber pistol as well. Her house was left in disarray, yet nothing was stolen and there was no forcible entry. Just recently I had the FBI do a spectrograph and comparison of the bullets removed from Mrs. Jacqueline Phyliss Moore's head and from the head of Mrs. Gloria Goldman. You wouldn't believe the coincidence; they both matched."

Spaulding was sitting on the sofa with his head bent down, clasping his hands together and sweating profusely.

Amanda continued. "Tomorrow morning at 9 o'clock two police officers will be at your office with a warrant for your arrest for multiple homicides. We are also in the process of investigating another murder from a few years before which follows the exact same pattern, but that doesn't interest me. Somehow all these automobiles wound up in your possession and you wound up with estate properties at a mere fraction of their wholesale value, let alone market value. Now here is your option, and it will never be repeated. You will sell Hampton Court including all its contents to Robert for $750,000 because he was such a great friend of yours for many years. The $300,000 in fees that you collected from Robert will be his down payment leaving a $450,000 balance. You will finance that $450,000 for 25 years at a 5% rate. Since Robert has been your dear friend for many, many years you are taking out a life insurance policy in the amount of $450,000 for double indemnity in the event of your demise, payable to Robert Snyder. All the automobiles that you have, except your three modern automobiles, will be handed over to Robert free and clear in exchange for the $150,000 worth of cars that he gave you at settlement. You will rent to Robert your garage on Fitzwater Street for $200 a month with a ten-year lease and no escalations. Would you care for a glass of Chardonnay or another Chevis Regal?"

William Aaron Spaulding Esquire sat there with his right hand on his chest and his heart palpitating. He had a choice to make. Either accede to her demands or be arrested in the morning.

"What assurance do I have that you still don't prosecute me?"

"I'm sorry, Bill. I forgot to tell you that I'm going to give you both the bullets I have in my possession. As far as anyone is concerned they are just two unsolved cases. Please take your time and think about it. You have one minute!"

"How soon can we complete this?"

"So you are accepting option two with the 'Get Out of Jail Free' card?"

"Yes. I will start drawing up the documents when I get back home tonight and hopefully by noon tomorrow they'll be ready. Is that acceptable to you Ms. Dillington?"

"Certainly, Bill. Now I insist that we have a toast to your freedom and the fair outcome for Robert Snyder."

Epilogue

Two weeks after the settlement of Hampton Court and the assignment of all the antique cars free and clear to Robert Snyder, Amanda and Robert decided to get married. Robert now had the comfort of knowing that he wasn't going to be living off of Amanda's income and thus there was no need to wait until he graduated law school.

It was their mutual desire to be married at Hampton Court. Amanda wanted to see a fresh start for both of them and the same for their lovely estate. They hired excellent painters from the area to freshen up their new home in anticipation of having a wonderful wedding there and a lifetime together of joy and happiness.

Stasha was called and interviewed by Amanda and was hired full time and glad to be back at Hampton Court.

Victor was contacted and given the position of property manager and also placed in charge of Robert's new auto collection. Robert and Amanda decided to give Victor the carriage house apartment free of any rental so he did not have to worry about having to live in a questionably unsafe neighborhood any longer.

Joanne, the physical and massage therapist, left Chaz Galloni and made weekly visits along with another competent massage therapist to give Amanda and Robert couples' massages.

Billy Thompson was released from prison on good behavior after serving six months. Through Amanda's contacts, she was able to get him an excellent job working for an antique dealer in Center City. He had changed his life and this was his fresh start.

When the painting contractors arrived they placed drop cloths over the floors to protect them and set up temporary framing to hold all the paintings that were to be removed from the walls. Behind one large painting was a hidden Yale safe. It seemed as though no one knew it was there. Amanda contacted a source who arrived at the property the following day spending three hours drilling before opening it.

Inside were $500,000 worth of bearer bonds and a bevy of jewelry. Bearer bonds were the same as cash since they were payable to whoever held them.

When an overjoyed Robert went to the garage he rented on Fitzwater Street, he noticed that something was missing. He asked the cleanup person who was now his part-time employee, "Where is the Mercedes Gullwing?"

He was told that it was never at the shop.

A few days later at William Spaulding was working underneath the Mercedes Gullwing which he had hidden from Robert and Amanda since this was his favorite car. Someone entered and from beneath the car Bill asked, "Who's there?"

No one answered. The garage entry door was open and all he could see peering out from beneath the automobile were a pair of legs walking by.

"Who's there?" he asked again, never to receive an answer. The person approached the right front wheel next to one of the four antique car jacks supporting the Mercedes and leaned on it throwing it off balance.

Appearing in all the news media the following day:

Highly Renowned Attorney's Accidental Death
Well known and highly respected attorney William Aaron Spaulding Esquire, partner of Calhoun, Spaulding, and Fiengold met his tragic death while working on his favorite classic automobile, a 1956 Mercedes-Benz Gullwing. It was determined that one of the car jacks that he used collapsed, crushing him to death. Everyone who knew him mourns his passing.

Finis

Gene Epstein

Author photo by Marlene Epstein

Gene Epstein has enjoyed a lifelong love of automobiles, as evidenced in his hilarious autobiography, *Lemon Juice, The Confessions of a Used Car Dealer - a metamorphosis.* He's exhibited many magnificent classic cars at prestigious automobile shows across the country. Generous by nature, his philanthropic projects have been featured on national and international television networks. In 2010, he was highlighted as the "Person of the Week" on CBS and in the Huffington Post as "The first Greatest Person of the Day" for his program "Hire Just One." Many economists consider that he was the catalyst who led the way out of the Great Recession. He and his bride, sweethearts since childhood, live in the Keystone State.

Made in the USA
Middletown, DE
28 June 2020